The Handywoman Stories

The Handywoman Stories

Lenore McComas Coberly

Swallow Press / Ohio University Press
Athens

Swallow Press/Ohio University Press, Athens, Ohio 45701
© 2002 by Lenore McComas Coberly
Printed in the United States of America
All rights reserved

Swallow Press/Ohio University Press books are printed on acid-free paper ⊗ ™

10 09 08 07 06 05 04 03 02   5 4 3 2 1

Frontispiece: Elizabeth Benforado

The following stories in this collection have been published in periodicals:
    "Going Over" in *Aura,* University of Alabama
    "Garnet" in the *Piedmont Review*
    "Will's Valentine" in *Byline*
    "The Fellowship at Wysong's Clearing" in *Short Fiction by Women*
    "Night-Blooming Cereus," "Sweet Shrub," "The Fellowship at
    Wysong's Clearing," "The Handywoman," and "The Death of Alma
    Ruth" in *Bibliophilos*

Library of Congress Cataloging-in-Publication Data

Coberly, Lenore M.
  The handywoman stories / Lenore McComas Coberly.
    p. cm.
  ISBN 0-8040-1044-7 (alk. paper)—ISBN 0-8040-1041-2 (pbk. : alk. paper)
  1. West Virginia—Fiction. I. Title.

PS3553.O227 H36 2002
813'.54—dc21   2001055126

Contents

Acknowledgments

No book is published without much encouragement. I am indebted to Marcia Preston, Rachel Whalen, and Professor Gerald Bobango, who chose to publish some of my stories in their journals. My Wednesday Writers Group listened with humor as well as sympathy toward the characters when the stories were new, and David Sanders, director of Swallow Press/Ohio University Press, paid me the valuable honor of telling me how much he enjoyed reading them. I cannot imagine the stories becoming a collection without his help.

When the final copy before printing came from Nancy Basmajian, manuscript editor, she said she cried and laughed while editing the book, sometimes at the same time, after which she spent several pages citing the Chicago Manual. That, I submit, is perfection in a copyeditor.

My greatest debt is to my relatives in Lincoln County who have received me with love and, always, humor through the years and to those all of us remember with the same love and humor. My children and grandchildren have pleased me by liking my stories, and Nina, my daughter-in-law, has made a scrapbook of my work. It is hard to live up to such faith, but when I falter, my husband and best friend, Cam, is there. No woman, even a handy one, is complete in herself.

The Handywoman Stories

Going Over

There was this she saw, he was wild. There was this she knew, she loved his wildness.

They ran through woods, kissed under needle-dripping pines, ate pawpaws on the sunny side of the hill, drank from shaded springs in noontime heat, before he went to find the boys at the still.

She waited, worked at washboard and stove, till night fell and he came, sad, lost in a remorse she could not know but felt in her beaten body. As dawn broke through the muslin curtain he found himself, in her.

There was this she saw, the child would live and not be wild. There was this she knew, he would love the child as he loved her.

She sang, "Jesus our Savior came forth for to die for poor ornery people like you and like I." He heard, "blessed are the poor in spirit . . . put your sins on the Lord . . . the preacher will lead you over."

He went over and their babies were safe. He was strong against dancing and drinking and kissing in the woods. She thanked the church and her Lord and dreamed of pawpaws ripe in the sun and pines shedding soft needles. Sometimes when dawn broke through the muslin curtain she awoke to wildness.

She could not know, but history would record that women on the American frontier used the church to civilize the men.

Garnet

I would slip across the road and watch Hobe Woodall's four daughters get dressed and made up, and sometimes they would give me a nearly empty powder box or cold cream jar. I thought they were beautiful. Besides, they were in high school when I was only in the first grade, and even then I knew they were not as beautiful as Mrs. Woodall. She had bright hair like broom sage where the light would shine on it. It lay around her face in soft waves and, when she talked, she sometimes twisted a piece of it between her thumb and finger. I tried to copy that gesture but my limp hair remained stubbornly straight.

There was a lot of talk that summer on our front porch, mostly about Mrs. Woodall. Somehow, I came to know that the silent Hobe Woodall was at fault but I didn't know how. I could see that Mrs. Woodall was going to have a baby and I cried when my mother told me she had died right after giving birth to her first son, Walter John. Mother was firm when she told the other women they should remember that Mrs. Woodall actually died of a stroke, but they were still mad at Mr. Woodall.

At the Baptist Church Mrs. Lucas played "Rock of Ages" on the piano while we went up to see Mrs. Woodall in her casket. My mother cried but everyone said the Woodalls held up well.

Everybody wondered what Mr. Woodall would do with Walter John. Two of the girls were fixing to get married to men who lived nearly thirty miles away and the other two wouldn't stay single long, the women agreed on that.

The day after the funeral Mr. Woodall got into the McJunkin Supply Company truck he drove to take tools to the drillers at the wells up Mud River and left town without a word. When he came back he had the skinniest woman I had ever seen on the truck seat beside him. She had straight hair cut level with the bottoms of her ears. Her dress was made from material we knew came as flour sacks. It didn't have any shape of its own and she didn't give it any. Her shoes were nearly worn-out oxfords and they were caked with mud around the soles.

My mother found it necessary to go out and clip grass on the outside of our fence just as they drove up, and Mr. Woodall said, "This here is Garnet." Mother said, "Hello, Garnet," and Garnet showed two black teeth just before she put her hand over her smile.

It wasn't long before we quit hearing Walter John crying and pretty soon even the yard was swept at the Woodalls'. By the time Walter John was walking, the girls were all gone.

The women wondered about when Garnet got up in

the morning, or if she ever went to bed. By eleven o'clock she would have her washing, cleaning, gardening, ironing, and canning done and be ready to fix a big noon dinner for Mr. Woodall before she started sewing. Her garden was full of green beans, potatoes, onions, beets, cucumbers, and watermelon. In the spring, before it got too hot, she would have lettuce and radishes in a bed covered with cheesecloth. She dried and canned beans, stored potatoes under the house, pickled beets and cucumbers, and made preserves out of the melon rind. All of this we knew because every day she would come to our house after Mr. Woodall had eaten and sit on our porch steps, bringing samples of what she had made. Mother would exclaim over it with sincerity because it was always delicious. Garnet would smile behind her hand.

Our houses were on the top of the first rise with the big hill going up behind our house on the north. Behind the Woodalls', just beyond Garnet's garden, was a sand hill we liked to slide down. Mr. Garfield Lovejoy, the school principal, lived at the bottom, and we tried to slide all the way to his back door just to hear him and Mrs. Lovejoy say, "Did you see that bird fly by out there?" or "I think that airplane is flying too low!" We would laugh and say it was just us and Walter John would smile Mrs. Woodall's sweet smile behind his hand.

People eventually figured out that Hobe Woodall had gone up a hollow off the Mud River Road and told the poor people living up there that he needed a girl to do his work. They offered to trade their girl Garnet for the used drilling tools in the truck. The deal was made but no one could find out how much McJunkin charged him for the old tools. The women said that was some bargain and maybe more of a bargain than you could see. Mother put a stop to this talk and said Garnet was well named. She was a jewel, Mother said, and any woman loved by children was a good woman.

In the evening Garnet and Hobe would sit on his front porch, she on the steps and he in a rocking chair. Sometimes we would hear him reading the newspaper out loud.

If you went down our hill to the west you went through broom sage and blackberry brambles. A creek came down the hill and passed through this high valley. Beyond the creek was another round rise that had been given by some Charleston people for a graveyard. My grandfather said they could afford to give it, they owned half of these hills. Mrs. Woodall was buried a little way below the top of the graveyard. The women said there was room in the Woodall lot for Mr. Woodall and Walter John.

Down by the creek at the bottom of the graveyard there was a big pignut tree. Pignuts are hickory nuts not fit for people to eat, but pigs just love them. Mr. Adkins and his boys had put a fence around the tree and they kept their hogs there. I liked to go high up on the hillside and walk down the creek. There were grapevines for swinging, green mosses, and early spring flowers. Later in the summer it was a place to cool off. One day I was sitting just above the pignut tree among some rocks with my feet in the water when I heard someone talking. I looked between the rocks and saw Hobe Woodall and Garnet standing by the pigpen.

"This is a good place for hogs, Garnet. Jerome Adkins said we could keep one here if you would help with the butchering. I said you didn't have much to do in December. Is that all right?"

She smiled and I thought I saw gold in her mouth. Then she reached her hand to his outstretched one. They stood there for a long time looking at the hogs, then she picked up a lard bucket and went over to the blackberry patch. He walked on down the creek toward the road.

I never told anyone about seeing them. It was a secret I liked to think about by myself. When I left for college, Garnet made an afghan for my room. Before I graduated, Mr. Woodall was dead and buried near the top of the second rise beside Mrs. Woodall.

Sometimes in the summer I would go back to visit and always Garnet would call "Howdy" from the still perfectly swept Woodall yard. My cousin wrote that Walter John married, then had a stroke, and died just like his mother. They said Garnet didn't cry but they had never seen her with her hand in front of her mouth again. Walter John's wife put him in her family's lot on the far side of the graveyard.

Last year I got to wondering about Garnet and I walked up to the graveyard to see what was on her stone. But the space beside Hobe Woodall was still empty. Down the hill, toward the pignut tree, at the very edge of the graveyard there was a grave by itself. Violets and wild roses bloomed close to it. At the head was a stone engraved, "This stone cut by Hobe Woodall for the grave of Garnet when her time comes, June, 1937." The stone looked familiar, like the ones

I used to sit on by the creek, not like gravestones from Italy or Indiana, and it was a deep red, dark and quiet as if it were shadowed by the big hill. It was, I suddenly knew, like garnet.

Over Sulphur Mountain

John had been teaching at Sulphur School for ten years but he still got a thrill riding up over Sulphur Mountain. His dad had told him to imagine whether Jesus would travel with him on a road he found himself traveling. John felt that the Sulphur Mountain road would be one Jesus would like but he was never really sure Jesus was there with him.

Most of the children he taught never went over the mountain. He often told them over-the-mountain stories about trains, cars, and stores that had all the goods you see in the Montgomery Ward catalogue out where you could touch them, even try them on. He wasn't sure they believed these stories the way they believed *The Trail of the Lonesome Pine* or *Hans Brinker and the Silver Skates* that he read from every Friday afternoon. He smiled remembering Henderson Brumfield, crowded into a desk chair that was way too small for him, listening to every word, his eyes shining.

Then, up ahead on the winding trail, he saw Harper Brumfield, Henderson's daddy, climbing up over a rocky ledge. "Howdy, Mr. Brumfield. How are you?" he called.

"Well, if it hain't the school man. Heared you want my boy to learn readin'."

"Yes, I came by your house a few weeks ago. Henderson wants to learn and he will work hard. He is over twelve years old." Seeing the set of the other man's jaw, ambeer running from the corner of his mouth, John decided to take a chance. "Why, little Clint Lucas is reading and he is only six."

The Brumfields and Lucases had had a blood feud as long as anyone alive could remember. John didn't believe any of them remembered what it was about but, remembering the look on Mrs. Brumfield's face when he told her Henderson was learning to read, John found the courage to nudge the big man.

"Hell, I don't care what any damn Lucas is doing. My boy hain't havin' anything to do with any Lucas!" He abruptly turned his back on John and started down the trail toward Sanging Creek.

John was hard to anger but he knew how fast children grew and what a short time there was to help them. "Well, the Democrats don't have anybody up here except me who can read to work the polls. Too bad Henderson can't read. Tom Lucas is a Republican, of course." He was hollering over his shoulder as he rode up the trail, rocks rolling under his horse's feet. Old man Brumfield would hear him. Some said he could hear federal revenuers when they got off the train on the other side of the mountain and get his still taken apart before they got there. Of course, that was a mountain tale but it had a grain of truth.

John was getting hot and would have liked to take off his tie but he tried not to let any of the families see him not dressed right. They needed all the pride he could teach them. Of course, Mayme made it possible, ironing white shirts and pressing pants for him. She knew why he wore them. It was for their five little ones the same as for the other mountain children.

Just over the top of the mountain in a laurel thicket there was a spring of the best water John had ever tasted. The day had gotten hot and he was glad to scoop handfuls of the cold water and let it run over his wrists before he drank his fill. He told Mayme once that he wished he could pipe that water to their house. The water from their dug well tasted and smelled of sulphur. "But it is good water! Sulphur is good for you," she had cried. How she loved this wild place. She had grown up here and was related to a lot of the people along the creek. He would be teaching down at the county seat if he hadn't met her at the teacher's institute. When he was alone, like today, he often remembered how they met and fell in love. It made the time fly.

Fry, a town of one shack of a store with house attached, was on the road to Logan, and coal trains went by every day. They brought the mail and the supplies John needed for school. He got some coffee at the store and a bag of penny candy for the children but he didn't linger to talk with the old men there. It was a long trip back over the mountain.

The children were waiting when he got to the creek even though shadows were gathering in the narrow valley.

Juliet and Hope, seven and nine, were too grown up to beg a ride but he hoisted little Tom and Fult onto the horse in front of him. He gave the bag of candy to the girls to carry carefully up the lane to the log house, beautiful to him every time he saw it.

Aunt Jule was on the porch waiting for the *Midkiff Republican* she knew he would bring. "Well, Aunt Jule, there is some real news this time," he called. "Here, Fult, take the horse out to the barn. See if Uncle Milt will help you rub him down." John often wondered how they would get along without his wife's aunt and uncle to help make a living.

"Yes, sir!" the five-year-old cried, pride in his voice and his skinny erect body.

Mayme came out onto the porch carrying the baby and asked, "What news, John?"

"Not before a kiss, Mayme!" he grinned and bent to kiss her flushed cheek and then threw himself down on the porch floor at Jule's feet. "Watch out, I'll rock on you," the old woman admonished, but he knew she liked being the first to hear news.

"Well, Franklin D. Roosevelt is coming all the way across Sulphur Mountain!"

"John, you fool," Mayme laughed, "you'll say any-thing."

"Well, of course I mean his programs, not actually him." The girls giggled and came to sit by him. "What is actually going to happen is that the WPA is going to build a road over Sulphur Mountain."

"Well, 'pon my soul," Jule murmured. Mayme looked doubtful

"Might make a Democrat out of Aunt Jule," John joked.

"Tell us what is going on, John," Mayme demanded.

"That's about all I know, but it will happen. Men will come from Midkiff and hire Sanging Creek people to work. You do wonder, don't you, who will use that road." They all had to do some thinking about this before they talked any more.

"Supper is ready, John. Better get washed." Mayme would know what she thought before bedtime. He looked forward to their whispered talk with her head on his shoulder, hands rubbing the tired out of him. He was a lucky man.

Pretty soon even Harper Brumfield was bragging about getting hired for the work crew, till he heard that Haley Lucas was going to be the foreman. He got really drunk after he heard that but didn't give up his job. Aunt Jule said that was progress.

Henderson kept coming to school when he could, but his ma needed him with Harper working on the road crew. When the crew got to the top of Sulphur Mountain and started down toward Sanging Creek, the schoolchildren could hear the pounding to break up rocks for the road before they could see the workers.

The Brumfields lived just under the edge of the mountain across the creek from the school. Henderson said rocks were falling down and hitting their house. Had his daddy so mad he was drunk part of the time.

"That won't help, Henderson," John told him.

"I know that, Mr. Ferrell," Henderson said, not looking up. John thought he was getting beaten down, like his mother.

The day of the shooting Henderson hadn't shown up at school, and when John heard shots from up the mountain he thought at once of Henderson. He told Hope to keep the children working and inside the school building. He ran across the creek, getting his pants wet to the knees, and met Mrs. Brumfield running down the path from their house. "Henderson killed him, Mr. Ferrell. I should not have called him. I should not. His daddy told me to call him. Haley Lucas had a shovel over Harper's head. He would have hit him." The distraught woman forgot to put her hands over her mouth as she usually did when she talked. John saw the black rotted teeth.

He put his hand on her shoulder and held tight to steady her. "You go on back home, Mrs. Brumfield. Let me talk to Henderson."

"They'll take him away. I cain't stand for him to be took away. He's a good boy." Tears were running down her face lined with sun and sorrow.

"Now, you go on back home. I'll go with him. I promise I will go with him." Hope came for a moment to her eyes and she turned back up the narrow path to the house in the hollow under the new road.

"Haley Lucas is dead, Mr. Ferrell," Henderson told him

when he got to where Henderson stood on a rock outcropping below the road.

"Maybe he isn't, Henderson. Did you shoot him?"

"Yes, sir, and he is dead. I never miss a squirrel's head and his was a sight bigger than that." There was a finality John knew well. He fought it in the mountain children every day. They did not believe in hoping.

The whole crew was gathered around Haley's body and he was dead all right, just as Henderson had said he would be. "The man from Midkiff has gone for the sheriff, Mr. Ferrell. He comes ever few days to see how we are doin' and he was here today tellin' Haley he had better get goin' faster on this here road."

"Did Haley and Harper fight?" John asked.

"No, sir, they jist shot words. Haley said it were Harper Brumfield's fault. Said Harper was drunk all the time. He took a shovel and started after Harper but then we heard a shot."

No one liked Haley Lucas and no one would accuse Henderson, John knew. "Henderson told me what happened," he said. They all looked at him and no one spoke. John thought this was a stillness uncommon even in the mountains. He heard the sound of water running over rocks and an occasional rock rolling down the hillside when a man shifted from one foot to the other. When the sheriff came just the Lucas family, John, and Henderson were there.

"Where are all of them?" Sheriff Sponaugle demanded.

"They all went home. Henderson here killed Haley Lucas. He told me all about it."

"Well, he'll have to tell a jury, not the schoolteacher!" John noticed that the sheriff was getting thick around the belly.

"I know that, Mr. Sponaugle," Henderson said, "and Mr. Ferrell is going with me."

"No he ain't, son, not this time. I'll take you to jail in Midkiff."

"I'll just ride along, Mr. Sponaugle," John said quietly, and there was no discussion.

As they neared the top of the mountain Henderson asked, "Mr. Ferrell, did your daddy ever tell you to do something you didn't want to do?"

John prayed to speak rightly. "Well, he told me to pick a road I was on and ask myself whether Jesus would go along that road with me."

"Did you ever find a road Jesus would go along?" They were nearly to the top of the mountain.

"Yes, Henderson, this road. Jesus will be with you all the way."

⁂

Henderson Brumfield was convicted of manslaughter and sent to the Moundsville State Prison. The teacher went with him to Moundsville and bade good-bye there. Five years later the teacher went back to Moundsville and assumed responsibility for Henderson on parole. Henderson never again went over Sulphur Mountain but he would sometimes ride just over the top to taste the sweet spring water found there.

Will's Valentine

The worst hurt I ever got in the State Police was during Prohibition when I tried to get a drunk woman out of the way of the law in a saloon. She stepped on my foot and her sharp high heel went straight through past the bone. Not that it amounted to much if you think of the whole of Lincoln County, but it does show how powerful women are and they don't even know it.

When I got through the state troopers' school in Charleston and they said I'd be going to Galloway down in Lincoln County, I wondered why they were punishing me. You need to know first thing that I am big and have red hair, thin but red. Anyway, I always have tried to be gentle like my folks taught me, because when you are big you can hurt someone. Partly I learned this from a female. I nearly got kicked in the head by a cow before I learned that if you use your full strength pulling milk, you won't get much milk.

But I did learn it. The stuff about redheads and temper is wrong. I have seen it over and over. My daddy was red-haired and he never scolded me in his life. He let me try out things for myself and carried me home when I needed it.

Now my mother was a bit different. She was a redhead, too, I guess, but her hair was brown with red where the light would shine on it. Daddy and I sometimes sat and looked at her head in the window light when she was working at the sink. She named me William Joseph and if anybody called me Billy Joe where she could hear it, you'd know why I said she was different. She would say, "If you don't know enough to speak politely, you don't know enough to eat at my table. Out." And she would hold the door open till the person she was talking to left. Same for swearing and making fun of people weaker than you.

When it came to making fun of people stronger than you, well, we were all good at that. We listened to Will Rogers on the radio and nearly died laughing. His humor suited the McCoughlins. Finally Ma settled for people calling me Will, but I was never Billy Joe.

Well, the day I first saw Galloway it was no surprise. The county courthouse rose on top of a middle-sized hill and the school sat on top of a low rise. The post office, Pa Hicks's store, the Hager Hotel, and Win Harper's Barber Shop were in between. Lawyers' offices were mostly on Court House Hill, and the funeral home, drugstore, Farmers and Merchants Bank, and the old building they showed Friday night movies in were down toward the river. People lived all between, but the Gillenwaters lived in a big stone house right across from the courthouse and next door to the Northern Methodist Church and parsonage. The State Police headquarters was in the jail building behind the courthouse, so that is how I came to walk by the Gillenwaters' so much.

Mrs. Gillenwater was tiny and fair, and people said she spent her share of Mr. Gillenwater's oil-drilling money on books and a piano. But she was plain dressed; Widow Elkins made her clothes out of material from Hicks's. I knew that because I saw a bit of the widow. She made the best chicken and dumplings you ever tasted.

Mrs. Gillenwater spoke to everybody, she was that plain. Her children played mostly in their big yard that stretched all the way down the back of Court House Hill. They had dogs and cats and a playhouse under a maple tree. Mrs. Gillenwater worked in her garden and played the piano at the Methodist Church.

When Jake Monday first told me he sure felt sorry for her, I thought she had TB or something. But later, after we got better acquainted and he quit acting like the old trooper with me the kid, I asked what he meant.

"Hell, Will, what is the matter with you? Old Gillenwater keeps a woman in a fancy house in Huntington. Has white rugs all over the floor and furniture made out of metal, I heard. I know who she is. Grew up over on Trace Creek. He went over there to drill and found more than oil. Everybody knows. I figure that's why Mrs. Gillenwater keeps her young'uns so close. Some women have it hard."

As time went on, I heard more about Mrs. Gillenwater, a lot more than I said, although I could have talked. I got acquainted with her when I did a program about the law for her Ladies Circle. They met at Gillenwaters' and served me chipped apple pie with homemade ice cream before I spoke. I tied West Virginia law in with the Old Testament. I tried to use Methodist understanding. The women liked me a lot. After that, one of them asked me to dinner every Sunday.

A few days after the meeting, Mrs. Gillenwater was working in her roses by the front fence when I walked by. She looked up and smiled. She wore a green checked dress with a white belt around her slim waist and her hair shone in the sun.

"Will, I want to thank you again for that program. It really woke up the women to think that they are equal to men under the law. You had to go pretty deep to find that in the Old Testament."

"Well, I guess the truth is it doesn't always work out fair." She lowered her eyes and I saw pink coming into her cheeks, but I stumbled on. "I mean, the law isn't perfect."

She smiled at me with her head at a slant. "You are certainly right about that. But what is?"

"Not me, I can tell you." I saw a glint of red in her hair where the sun played with it.

"Would you like a glass of lemonade and some pound cake? It's so hot today." She held the gate open and I walked onto the cool front porch and sat down on a swing with June, the youngest Gillenwater girl. She showed me her new book about *Little Women* after Jo grew up.

"You're some reader for only eight years old," I said.

She looked at me, with her head tilted, like her mama's, and said, "I read because I like to." With that she turned back to her book and I stretched my legs in my leather leggings out as far as they would go. I felt right at home by the little girl with her mother bringing cake that smelled of mace.

People talked about me, of course. I was that shy young policeman from up near Clarksburg and it was natural that I should spend my spare time helping out around the church and the parsonage. Sometimes over at Gillenwaters', too. The preacher's wife put her hand on my arm one day and said, "God will reward you for helping that poor woman. Her man treats her shamefully and her so helpless."

She was right about my reward, but not about the helpless part. One night we had just finished washing up after a church Valentine's Day dinner. Mrs. Gillenwater and I turned the lights out and started up the basement steps. She stumbled and nearly fell. When I caught her, I just forgot myself completely and kissed her. I mean I really kissed her. I thought I had gone to heaven till I heard people upstairs closing up the church.

"Mrs. Gillenwater," I started to mumble when she drew back her hand and slapped me. She hit me so hard my head slammed against the wall.

"Don't you *ever* call me that again." She marched straight-backed up the steps, called goodnight to the preacher, and went home to her children. I called her Rachel after that, and the bump on my head felt like a Valentine.

In Which Murder Is Done

The sun came up as usual on February 15 and Crede Gillenwater kept pumping money out of the laurel-coated hills
around Galloway. Capt. Jake Monday sent me up on Mud to
check on Clyde Unger's kids. We knew there wasn't much
State Police could do, but I went anyway. The teacher said
those kids were coming to school black and blue.

Mrs. Unger was out front cranking the wringer on an
old washing machine. "Howdy," she said when I got to the
rock that served as porch steps.

"Morning, Mrs. Unger. Nice day for February, isn't it?"

"Depends," she said, lifting a heavy basket of wet
clothes from behind the washer.

"Here, let me carry that for you. You hang them in the
backyard?"

"Ain't no backyard. The hill is there. Spread them out
here."

Soon the porch rail, wild rose bushes, and even the
laurel and rocks by the spring running out of the mountain
were festooned with ragged diapers and unbleached muslin
sheets with flour sack labels here and there. She told me

not to use the posts. They were for tying up the hunting dogs.

"I came to find out if we could help you about your children, Mrs. Unger. Miss Lavonia is worried."

"Miss Lavonia is a good teacher," she commented, eyes averted. I knew one of her eyes wandered around under its own power sometimes so I looked sort of sideways when I talked to her.

"Who is hurting them, Mrs. Unger? Is it their daddy?" I took the chance that he wasn't around because the dogs were gone.

She was looking down at her red raw hands and I saw a tear fall on one of them. "Ain't no one hurt them young'uns. Just leave us be."

"I know you can't talk about it. Just nod your head when I ask questions." Foolish, I knew. She was scared for her children. If he killed her where would they be?

Then she looked up at me, her face like a wild dying thing, the one eye darting sightless to and fro. "Tell Miss Lavonia to keep them!" She stumbled up the steps and into the raw board shack that was all she knew of home. I stood there for a while and then drove slowly back to Galloway.

"Well, did you see Clyde Unger?" Jake asked, soon as I walked in.

"No, I did not, but I saw Mrs. Unger and she said we should keep the children down here."

"What do you mean?"

"That's what she said, and I am going to fix it so we can."

"Wait a minute. What about Hal? You didn't ask him."

"He's a drunk and a murderer. You know that."

"Have you ever tried proving that in court?"

"No," I admitted, "but I know it."

"Be careful, son. Go ahead and talk to Miss Lavonia and Mr. Guy, the principal. You know him?"

"Yes," I said as I walked out into the sun and wind of coming spring. I didn't say I thought Mr. Guy wouldn't be much of a match for Clyde Unger.

Well, Miss Lavonia said I had made progress by just getting Mrs. Unger to face up to the danger to her children. "Let me think about it," she said.

Rachel Gillenwater said of course the children could stay at her house. She got Preacher Priestly to call a meeting to collect money for their books and clothes. I helped her, a lot, and didn't give a thought to Crede Gillenwater coming home from Huntington where his other woman lived. That's why Rachel and I were sitting side by side at the dining room table trying to get the record of contributions straight when he walked in the back door.

"Who the hell is this, Rachel?" He sounded only slightly interested.

"This is Will McCoughlin. Works with Jake Monday in the State Police Force." Rachel didn't touch me but I could feel her hand and I knew Gillenwater knew I could.

"Working overtime, Trooper?" I could see the tendons on Rachel's neck tighten. I stood up with her partly behind me.

"No, sir. Your wife is helping us see that children who are temporary wards of the state have the clothes and school supplies they need."

"Is she now? Well, just who are these wards of the state?"

"Some children the teacher found had been beaten."

He threw back his head and laughed. "Just how many children up them hollers do you figure haven't been beaten, Mr. McCoughlin?"

"I don't know, sir, but it isn't right and we have to protect the children." I sounded like a weasel even to myself.

"Protect the children! Just who do you think you are protecting them from?"

I could see the steel blue between his squinted eyelids and knew I would fight this man. "From anyone who hurts them," I said.

"Hurts! My God, hurts! Life hurts! You are talking about ignorant people who depend on people like me just to even keep from starving. Those children have a lot to learn!"

I knew that what he said was true but I couldn't bear to know it. I saw Mrs. Unger's red hands, ten-year-old Eddie Bill's legs bleeding through his pants. What was he learning? "We don't need to talk anymore about this, Mr. Gillenwater. Thank you for your help, Mrs. Gillenwater." I didn't look at her but I had called her the name she hated most.

As I left the house I heard Crede Gillenwater laugh and speak loudly for my benefit. "You come here to Daddy, Baby

Girl. I need some sugar—" I hurried through the gate and over to the office. I told Jake I needed to ride around a while. He said to go ahead.

I had just gotten to the office next morning when the call came. Jake answered and wrote down the message and handed it over without looking at me. Crede Gillenwater had been shot and he died before they got him to the hospital. Jake got his hat and told me to come with him.

"I want to go and see Rachel," I protested.

"You come with me," he ordered in a voice I knew was final.

On the way up Mud River Jake asked, "Where were you last night?"

"Home in bed," I said. "Why?"

"Anybody see you?" He looked straight at the road.

"You think I was sleeping with somebody?"

"Anybody see you go up to your apartment?"

"My apartment is over a garage. Old Mrs. Pridemore doesn't pay much attention to me unless she wants something fixed. I didn't see her last night."

"Anybody on the street. Did you say howdy to anybody last night?"

I was beginning to see. I was a suspect. How I wished there was a reason! "Look, Crede Gillenwater was not jealous of me. He had no reason!"

"Depends, doesn't it? Did he think he had a reason?"

"How do I know what he thought? What are we doing, Jake?" He had still not looked at me.

"We are going to where Gillenwater's body was found, and you had better be telling me the truth." That was all he said till we stopped out by the spring below Unger's shack. There wasn't anybody in sight but I knew Mrs. Unger was watching us.

"Shouldn't we go up to the house?" I asked.

"Not yet. Show me where the body was."

I looked at Jake in amazement. "How would I know, and if I did know, would I be dumb enough to admit it?"

"Yes, you would. Come on, we have to comb the area around the spring."

The weeds were mashed down and matted with blood at the edge of the woods. The body had been under the laurel cover. "The question is," I said, "how did it get under the laurel to start with?"

"Had to be carried. No sign of dragging. Else he was killed there, but I don't see any broken branches."

"Laurel bends. It doesn't break. You could strip it, though." I walked around the laurel clump right into the business end of Clyde Unger's rifle.

"Stay right there, both of you. Throw them pistols on the dirt," Unger growled. We backed into the clearing but not before I saw something move further back in the woods. "I didn't kill that son-of-a-bitch. Came here drinking my brew. Wants me to sign a lease for him to take oil out of my land. Make money—" Then he grinned. "Anyway, last night I got some real money out of him. Knew what he wanted."

The slim figure came out of the woods silently. Neither of us saw what she had in her hand. When Clyde turned to where we were looking I jumped on him and felt a rifle shot beside my foot. Then I collapsed under Clyde's weight and felt the sickening snap of my ribs before I blacked out.

Mrs. Unger was still holding the heavy black iron skillet when I came to and she was screaming, "I killed him. I killed him! What will happen to the young'uns?"

Jake went over to her and gently took the skillet out of her hand. "It was self-defense, Mrs. Unger, and you saved our lives, too. Don't cry. We'll take you down to Miss Lavonia. She'll know what to do. Help me get Will into the truck."

Supported between them I got my legs to work. Mrs. Unger was a lot stronger than I had figured. When I got into the truck seat she said, "I have to go back and get my baby."

We sat waiting till she came back and climbed into the back of the truck. Breathing was hurting me a lot so I couldn't protest.

"Why isn't Eddie Bill at school?" Jake yelled back at Mrs. Unger. She didn't answer. Maybe she couldn't hear.

"How do you know he's not at school, Jake?" I asked. Just then I saw the skinny, barefoot kid watching us from the limb of a sycamore tree on the lower side of the road.

"The oldest son has to take care of his mother and God knows his mother needed care."

When I went up onto the Gillenwater porch little June came out and told me her mother did not want to see me. "Tell her I'm sorry about your daddy," I mumbled and nearly fell backwards stumbling toward the steps.

Jake looked at me when I got back to the office and snorted. "Went for a condolence call, did you? Looks like it didn't go too well."

"I can't help being stupid, Jake."

He stopped writing a report and came over to me. "Will, you are not stupid. You are good and you are young. Slow down."

"Slow down! Want me to be alone like you?" I couldn't believe I had said that. Why should I hurt Jake?

"Sit down, Will." Jake took a bottle out of the bottom drawer of his desk. He had never let me see this before but I always knew it was there. He took a long drink and handed it to me. "No, thanks," I mumbled. Jake put it back in the drawer.

"Don't expect a lot of credit, Will, just for hanging around the least of them."

"You don't pay any special attention to children, Jake."

"I don't just mean children, Will. I mean the trash, the drunks, the have-nots that live on Left Fork. Do you think they are that way because they want to be?" He took another drink from the bottle. His hands were beginning to tremble and his eyes were watery. I didn't know what to say. For once, I knew how dumb I was.

After a long time Jake looked at me and said, "I think Mrs. Unger and the kids ought to live in that apartment you have. They can take care of Mrs. Pridemore and she can enjoy them."

"And where am I supposed to live?" I was tired of being pushed around.

"You can board at Hager's." He just sat looking out the window. For once, I had enough sense to wait.

❋

When we made out the report on Crede Gillenwater's murder we said it was probably Clyde Unger but we didn't report what he said just before he got hit on the head with that skillet. Besides, Eddie Bill was too young to prosecute and we didn't want to know what Crede was doing to Eddie Bill's mama before he died. He and Clyde were probably both drunk. All the people up the hollow would consider it good riddance. Jake was satisfied.

"I can't leave it like this, Jake."

"Then you will be glad to know that I can have you transferred."

"I didn't ask for a transfer."

"That is not how it works, Will."

"You are jealous of me, Jake. You are going after Rachel. I've seen you looking at her. You're old, Jake!" I was shouting but he just sat slouched in his chair and looked at me.

"She was Rachel Swanson, Will. You didn't know that, did you? We were engaged, sort of, but she married Crede thinking she could save him. The damned stupidity and goodness of women! Doesn't it kill you, Will?"

I saw Miss Lavonia's old car in the lane and she was out in the back hacking at ragweed six feet tall with a sickle. I slipped and slid straight down the hill and yelled at her. "Miss Lavonia, let me do that. You need a scythe."

"I don't have a scythe, Will. All you have to do is hack down one weed at a time." I didn't argue and took the sickle from her. Then I got out my pocketknife and began cutting them at the ground. She laughed and said, "All right, Will. There are some old tools in the barn but you'll have to sharpen them. It's too late to do a job like this today. Let's sit out on the porch and soak up the late sun." I was ready.

We were quiet for a long time with the sun getting lower over beyond the covered bridge and the shadows of the sycamore getting longer by the river. We went in to have her mother's hot biscuits and chicken just after I called her Vonia and she smiled. "Not in front of the children, though, Will."

The Sighting

The morning of the sighting Mr. Adkins came over early enough for one of Mama's biscuits and told me to get my coat.

"Sit down and have a biscuit, Mr. Adkins," Mama said soothingly, "and have some plum butter."

"There is not any time. Miss Lavonia, you have got to come right now."

Now, this is not the way people in Galloway usually act. If we don't have time to visit a little bit we stay by ourselves, out of sight. So I got my coat.

"What in the world has happened? Has that Gillenwater boy climbed up the corner of the house and got stuck on the roof again?"

"I'll try to tell you while we run, Miss Lavonia. We have got to hurry."

He headed us up the hill toward the old Whittaker place that was on the very top. No one knew when the Whittakers left there but we knew the first one came when these hills were covered with timber and there wasn't any mill, or school, or courthouse. Now the old chimney is just a pile of rocks with wild rose growing all over it. But I liked to take my class up there for school picnics so they could feel the feel of being on top.

Well, going up that hill fast doesn't aid conversation but even Mr. Adkins has mountain lungs. "This morning I was out in the road in front of my house checking the weather and I saw something settling into the trees just over the old Whittaker place and it disappeared and I didn't see it again." Then I heard the school bell and realized that I had to get back down that hill in a hurry. Mr. Adkins wasn't stopped by the bell. He went on, "It was round like a big saucer and I told my boy, Bobby, and we wondered." Bobby usually stopped at the wondering stage, but I didn't say so.

"You are getting tired, Mr. Adkins. Why don't you just rest on this rock and I'll be right back. I see Trooper Will at the bottom of the hill."

"That's because I called the State Police," Mr. Adkins pronounced. I didn't bother to say that it is irresponsible to take police time for superstition.

When Trooper Will caught up with me I said we wouldn't need any help. "Everybody can use help, Miss Lavonia," he said. "Preacher White has said many times that none of us knows everything."

"Well, in his case, that is gospel." Then Will and I had to laugh together. Actually, I have noticed that we laugh a lot.

Elijah Fisher, the jailkeeper, caught up with us and said he had to find out what was going on so he could tell his prisoners. Only fair, them locked up and all. We said he was uncommonly considerate, but he was already worn out so why didn't he go up and sit for a while with Mr. Adkins. We'd be back.

Will said he would help me lead the children in my class up on the hill.

"How did you know I was going to do that?" I asked, surprised.

"Because you want them to learn not to be superstitious."

It still surprised me that I was teaching in the same school my mama had taught in. It isn't as though Galloway is a great place to live. In fact, the only new people who ever move here are state policemen like Will McCoughlin who can't say no to a first assignment. It's funny that since I have known him I have seen us as more interesting and even likable. Of course, Will and I agree about the children and know how much they need us.

We got the children lined up out back of the school by the well. They were glad to see him because Mr. Adkins's story had gotten around town and they were scared. "Now, everybody get a partner and line up. I will lead with Geraldine and Trooper Will will follow us." I took the smallest girl's hand and headed up the hill. I didn't have to tell them to be quiet and orderly. Apprehension showed in their eyes and in the tenseness of their bodies.

The walk up the hill to the rock where Mr. Fisher and Mr. Adkins were sitting took only a few minutes. As we climbed we heard Mr. Adkins's story all over again until he ran out of breath. As we passed into the pine woods all of us, even those eleven little people, were so still we could hear our own footfalls on the dry pine needles. When we got to the old clearing the light came through openings slanted, like rays from angels, maybe, or the kind you see dust in right after you shake out your cushions. Then we saw him.

Standing there on top of the old chimney rocks was Edward Hager. He was handing up the biggest umbrella I ever saw to his brother, Vernon. Vernon was clear at the top of an old pignut tree trying to pull that umbrella up with a rope.

"Vernon Hager, what are you doing?" I demanded. "You are supposed to be in school."

"Miss Lavonia, I will be. I meant to be. I didn't mean to be late. We got up early. But this thing worked so well I wanted to fix it and try again."

"Worked so well. Again. You mean you flew to the ground with that umbrella made out of Bates bedspreads and rusted gas company pipe?"

"No, mam, I didn't. But it floated down by itself as nice as you please so me and Edward drew straws who would fly down with it. I won."

"'Edward and I drew straws,' Vernon. But you need to figure the weight it can hold before you try it. You need to make calculations."

"Yes, mam, Miss Lavonia." He came right down without another word and all of us headed back down the hill. Edward put the umbrella under some bushes, but we pretended not to notice.

"All of you want to stop at Ullom's Restaurant and have a biscuit?" Will invited. I said certainly not, we had wasted enough time already. Elijah Fisher said he might take him up on it. His inmates would wait. Besides, Mama had already invited Will for supper on Tuesdays and he never failed to come. Sometimes he even helps me mark papers because he went to Berea College like I did.

Night-Blooming Cereus

Alma Ruth is always suspicious that I'll stay home and miss everything so she offered to walk down to my house and go up to Aunt Addie's with me. I said not to be silly, Aunt Addie lived between us and there was no use in her walking down to my house. I didn't say so but this time she didn't need to push me.

I wasn't going to tell anyone that Junior Grass had said he'd be at Aunt Addie's to see her night-blooming cereus. He came by the house every few days and we just visited out on the porch or out back by the well. I reminded Alma Ruth that Junior and I were friends, had been ever since I sat beside of him at school, but my dropping out after my folks died made me seem a lot older than him. She laughed at that and said she was surprised I could still get around, at my age.

All the same, I did not consider us to be sweethearts until he told me what he didn't tell anyone else. He said he knew we were going to get into the war and he was joining the Marines. He went to Huntington and enlisted and he was leaving for Parris Island the day after Aunt Addie's cereus was set to bloom. Seemed like a sign, he said, and I said it did to me, too. He was drawing a bucket of water out of the well while he told me this, and I reached out and touched his hand. It was cool from the well and strong when it covered my hand. "I love you, Ruby Louise, I always have." Just like that.

It came to me that I had touched his hand first and what had I done? But I just stood there looking at him, with my heart pounding, till he bent his head and kissed me on the cheek. I wanted to reach out and hold him to me more than anything I have wanted in my life but I said, "I have to go in and do some cooking for the night-blooming cereus watch."

Seemed like he was sort of stumbling over his feet as he set the bucket over on the steps. He said he'd see me at Aunt Addie's and I said yes he would, God willing, and we laughed like I was a wit or something.

Well, I went up the hill to Aunt Addie's about nine o'clock and it seemed like everyone in town was there. "Now all of you just help yourself. Eat your fill," Aunt Addie was saying, "here comes Ruby Louise and you know what a cook she is."

"We sure do," Mr. John Mayhew Grass, Junior's daddy, laughed while he held the back door screen open for me. I set my stack cake and cold chicken on the dining room table and went into the front room to see the cereus.

Moonlight was coming in soft through the lace curtains and it glowed on the tin lard bucket Aunt Addie had set the cereus in. She told us it might need a tub before it bloomed again. People were out on the front porch with oil lamps lit and they made shadows coming and going through the front window and the screen door. I just stood there for a while finding where that flower was taking me.

It was white and big but it seemed to almost be part of the curtain behind it. Aunt Addie said it would be nearly midnight before it was clear open but it was filling the room with the smell of some island place that we had only read about. It was not of our mountains. Somebody said maybe it was from the Holy Land. Aunt Addie said she got the start from a woman who lived over on Coal River.

I could hear Junior out on the porch even though he was talking softly. I could have heard him whisper, I felt that close to him. After a while he looked in the door and told me it was nice and cool on the porch. I went out and we sat on the banister and listened while my grandpa told about what was happening in Europe. "We'll be in the war soon." Everyone gave a kind of solemn mumbled yes but I could tell Junior wanted to get away.

I stood up and walked down the steps and he followed me. Then, like it should happen on a night when magic is everywhere, he took my hand and we started on the upper path around the ridge that leads to the pawpaw patch on the south side of the hill. But we didn't go on around the hill. We stopped by some big rocks that were part covered with moss and chose a flat one to sit on where we could lean back and look out over the valley to the river and the covered bridge by Hilberts'.

"There is no place on earth like this, Ruby Louise," he said, bringing my head to his shoulder, his arm around me.

"That is the truth, Junior," I said, "but there will never be a time like this again either."

Everything that needed saying had been said. The rest was giving and receiving and knowing that we were alive and together and that there wasn't anything could ever change this time and this place for us.

When we got back everyone was crowded into Aunt Addie's little front room and no one was talking. The cereus was full open and it was easy to believe there was a light coming from it and, in its heart, we could see, just for an hour, the mother and child.

I woke up early like I had been doing ever since Pearl Harbor, and I said to myself that I had better slow down and think on things for a while. Even pray, if I felt the Spirit. Trouble was, one morning I started crying. That is not like me at all and that's one thing I won't tell Alma Ruth.

Alma Ruth would be over before nine o'clock to walk down to the post office but that was not all I needed. Every morning I got up before the chickens and worked as fast as I could. Faster than I had ever worked in my life before. I'd gather the eggs and clean them, hoe my garden, wash or iron or scrub my house, depending on the day, and have breakfast over before Alma Ruth got down the hill. Even in the evening we were doing our air warden duty.

A few weeks after Pearl Harbor Alma Ruth came over and said they needed volunteers for civil defense work. I said I wasn't much good at knitting but I'd bake cookies to send overseas. I could make them with sorghum. She said she didn't mean war work, she meant civil defense.

Well, it's hard to figure but before I knew it I was up at the courthouse drilling with Old Man Adkins, two of the Turley children who were in high school, John Mayhew Grass, and Alma Ruth. We tried to march together but we were so ill-matched we decided it was better just to do it at the same time but not necessarily together, if you see what I mean. When the weather got warm and we had the windows open the jailbirds would try to be funny about us. "Sure hope the wind don't blow. Might bring out the army." "Hey, Miss Ruby Louise, want to save my life?" All of which I ignored completely.

But we didn't just drill. We planned, too. People in Washington sent us a list of things to check every night if there was ever air raids over Hamlin. The first item was to turn out the street lights. That was easy. We didn't have any. But item ten said to have personnel available for emergency first aid and that was harder. Miss Conza went to Charleston and took a first aid course and came back and taught us. She remarked it made teaching the fifth grade look easy but we knew she was joking. I bandaged Alma Ruth and she bandaged me till we got so we couldn't look at a white rag without laughing.

Anyway, we were ready when the raid came even though it was in broad daylight. Mr. Adkins heard the plane first and saw it circling the town getting lower and lower. He ran, poor old soul had rheumatism, to Alma Ruth's and told her to call John Mayhew. Alma Ruth and I ran down to Belcher's garage and got our first aid kit open. But just then that plane came down so low we could see a man in the cockpit and it made a terrible sound. We fully realized, in that moment, that only God could save us in an air raid. We covered our ears and hunkered down under an old worktable with the mechanics. Well, the plane finally left without dropping a single bomb and we dusted ourselves off and went back to work.

That evening, when I went down to the post office for the evening mail, Mrs. Yeager was laughing and telling everyone that that was Charles buzzing the town. He was a flyer stationed down at Dayton, Ohio. I didn't mention going down to Belcher's garage because there was too much laughing anyway. John Mayhew caught most of the jokes because he said Charles ought to save gas to fight Germans. Mrs. Yeager said he needed to practice and we couldn't argue with that. We guessed if he could learn to sight Hamlin he could sight Berlin any day.

But, like I said, the time came when I wanted to stop for a while and think, or not think, if it felt better. All of us, after Pearl Harbor, just turned on all our cylinders, as Mr. Belcher once said. The kids in school studied harder, the women sewed faster, and we all gardened more. Store people kept longer hours, and I wouldn't be surprised if the men at Holley's Pool Hall didn't play more games. We didn't figure whether what we did helped the war effort, we just did what we knew how to do and did it more.

That's what I had to think through that day. What was it all about? But before I had been quiet for ten minutes, I was crying my eyes out. All I could think about was those four boys, our boys, Hamlin's boys, all dead at Bataan. They hadn't even found their bodies. Those boys never had time to find out where they were. We couldn't say the names of the places where our boys were dying. I would never know what the place where Junior died was like. I hope there were flowers there and that he could smell them. Maybe night-blooming cereuses grew there.

I heard Alma Ruth running down the road calling howdy to everyone along the way. I went out to the well and drew myself a really cold cup of water, took off my apron, and went to meet her so we could go to the post office. Someone had a letter from a fighting man in nearly every mail now.

I had four pies to bake for the Baptist Church Bake Sale. They were raising money for a new bell that could be used for civil defense purposes. We did what we could. That must be what the boys on Bataan thought, even the Japanese.

Early Transparent

Nelle

"Why does Nada Jo always walk home with Clint?" I asked, in exasperation, because it seemed to me they weren't having nearly as much fun as Nada Jo had when she stopped and played hopscotch with me. In fact, all they did was hold hands, with Nada Jo's books under Clint's arm. "Can't she even carry her own books?" I demanded.

"Well, I think," Mother answered slowly as her blue eyes turned past me to the Early Transparent apple tree that my father had planted before he was killed, "I'm pretty sure Nada Jo is a one-man woman." She went on stringing the beans on a torn paper sack on her lap and dropping them into a kettle on the floor. I liked to hear how they pinged at first when they hit the bottom of the kettle and plumed when the kettle began to fill.

"Are you a one-man woman, Mother? Is that why you never did marry Mr. Mayland or Mr. Dunbar or Hollie Holbrook? Mrs. Sweetland said all of them wanted to marry you."

She threw back her head and laughed so that Mrs. Sweetland across the road looked up from working in her garden and smiled across at us. "Don't believe everything you hear, dear child, but, yes, I think I was, am, and I hope you are, too."

"Why?"

"You'll see, you'll see."

After Clint carried Nada Jo's books up to her house at the end of the road going up the reservoir hill, he ran back down and across the football field to the gym for practice. He played everything but never was the star, just on the first team. "Still water runs deep," I heard Mrs. Sweetland say to Mother one time when he went by. He was best friends with Mrs. Sweetland's boy Hayes. He'd always call, "Howdy" and smile at me.

One time he asked me about what we did when Nada Jo played with me. I said we watched our mothers make apple butter or something and then I'd beat Nada Jo at hopscotch. After that, I said, we would look for four-leaf clovers but I was always the one who found some. Then we'd go over to Mrs. Sweetland's house and I would get her to give us sweet cakes. He said it was nice talking with me. I think it was, too.

They graduated in 1940 and Clint went to the Marines with three other town boys. We weren't in the war and Mrs. Sweetland told my mother what she thought. "Clint is foolish to go off like that. This isn't our war. Let England fight its own war. He'll lose Nada Jo, that's what will happen. You see if he doesn't." She shook her head, her mouth tight.

"I think you are wrong, Mrs. Sweetland. All our boys

will go. It's like the world is wrapped up in a whirlwind and we are all getting caught in it. Maybe we are making it at the same time." Her voice got soft and I didn't feel like speaking, only waiting for what she would say. I guess Mrs. Sweetland felt the same way. She just looked at Mother. "As for Nada Jo, no worry there for Clint."

Nada Jo got a job at Sweetland's store and saved her money. She showed me her bank book that Mr. Mayland put numbers in when she took her pay to the bank. The numbers got bigger and bigger. She said, "Clint will be home before long. All the boys will be. They're saving their money, too."

When Pearl Harbor happened Mrs. Sweetland said Mother had certainly been a prophet, she should have listened. When Clint and all three of the other boys got captured at some place called Bataan we all cried and watched poor little Nada Jo walk up the hill by herself every day.

Two years later the Red Cross notified the families that they were all dead. The whole town grieved and went to the funeral at the Baptist Church. We hadn't ever been to a funeral where there wasn't a body before but Preacher Parsons said we had to think of Clint's soul and how it was in heaven. Nada Jo came over that evening and sat on the porch with Mother. Mother told me to go to bed. I crept back down to the front room window and listened but it didn't do me any good. They just sat there together looking at the moon coming up. I could smell the blossoms on the Early Transparent tree.

Hayes Sweetland got hurt at a training base in Texas

and came back home a hero because he was our first returning serviceman. Mother said it would embarrass a man like
him but we had a church dinner welcoming him. When he
made his speech he said we ought to be thinking about the
boys still over there and about those who would never come
home, not even minus one eye like he had. That evening he
walked Nada Jo up the hill.

They were married that fall and she helped him study
for a post office job. As soon as he got settled she quit her
job and they had a little girl. You ought to have seen that
baby. Every woman in town said she had never seen such a
sweet baby. Hayes would beam from his one eye and Nada
Jo would bend over the baby to be sure she was all right.
She let me hold baby Lily sometimes.

Then the bomb was dropped on Japan and we didn't
know what to think. Mother said she felt sorry for Mr. Tru-
man. I just thought how strange it would be to have the boys
come home. But none of us figured on what happened.

The Red Cross got hold of Clint's family and told them
they had found Clint in a prisoner's camp in Japan. All of us,
even his mother, were afraid to tell Nada Jo. Hayes told her.

Nada Jo tried to divorce Hayes because she didn't know
what was true when she married him but Mr. Dunbar told
her she couldn't do that. She didn't have to anyway because
Hayes signed papers saying he was deserting her. All of us
knew it wasn't true.

She came out to our house and asked Mother if she
would take her to Huntington so she could get a train to
San Francisco to meet Clint's ship. Later Mrs. Sweetland

jumped on Mother and said she ought not to have helped a mother to desert her child.

"Mrs. Sweetland," my mother said and I thought she was like a Bible woman, maybe Deborah or Hagar, "every woman has to be true to herself. No one knows the hurt but her. And Lily is very lucky to have a grandma like you."

Mrs. Sweetland said she was going home and pick some rhubarb for supper. She looked at me and said she could use some help. We left Mother alone looking out at the Early Transparent tree.

Mrs. Sweetland

I watched Hayes moon over Nada Jo till I was almost sick. She was little and she was beautiful and she was smart but, like most of the girls in the county, she had eyes only for Clint. Hayes thought I didn't know and I let him, but his grandpa and I talked about it. Of course, his dad never noticed. He didn't notice much, come to think about it. Lucky in some ways, Dad was.

But I have to give him credit for wanting the best for Hayes. He saved money for his university tuition and let him have it when Hayes decided to go to Marshall College down at Huntington. Of course, Hayes could have gone anywhere on the GI Bill but he had only one thing on his mind—Nada Jo.

Her short curly hair would blow in the wind and still look good and she made good grades besides. But there were skinny straight-haired girls who were friendly and made good grades. What was it about Nada Jo? I guess Maud Fry's theory about her being a one-man woman might have been her attraction from the first. Men like to think they are special among men or else they want to be good guys among good guys. Clint wanted to be special and I guess Hayes did, too.

Hayes's daddy and I dreamed of him being a doctor or a lawyer someday. He made such good grades all through school we thought he could be anything. Not that we didn't know that who he married would make all the difference. It always does. But he seemed just to be good friends with everyone, especially with Clint and Nada Jo.

Seems dumb to me for her to choose Clint ahead of Hayes but I am Hayes's mother. Maud Fry across the road seemed to always understand. Maybe losing her man so young made her see things more clearly. Anyway, if anybody helped Nada Jo to leave Hayes it was Maud Fry. I try not to think about that but it is hard.

There is Hayes playing dominoes with little Lily when I know his heart is broken. He works at the post office and comes home. They can't even get him to Sunday School parties most of the time but he teaches a class on Sunday. I guess I should feel lucky having my son and little granddaughter here with me but I don't, not when I see his loneliness and she asks me why her mother doesn't come to see her. I don't have any trouble seeing why Hayes doesn't ever want to see Nada Jo. I don't either.

If he has any sense he'll start to notice that little Nelle

Fry isn't so little anymore. And she is happy like her daddy, not dreamy like her mother. But even Nelle always wanted to be with Clint. Maybe beautiful women can afford to be dumb.

Hayes

"Come on in here, Hayes, what are you doing out there?" My mother never needed answers to her questions, a fact I had figured out but still needed to do some wondering about, so I went in to supper. I couldn't have told her anyway that I was out there watching Nada Jo and Clint walking up the hill. I had watched Nada Jo as long as I could remember. She was so little, even now in high school, that she could stand under my arm. Clint took a picture of us standing that way at a Sunday School picnic one time. I had it under the glass on my dresser with enough other pictures so it didn't stand out to anybody but me.

Clint knew Nada Jo had played with me when we were little. We made roads in the mud for my toy trucks and cars when it rained and in the dust when it didn't. Sometimes Mrs. Petrie, Nada Jo's mama, would tell us playing out in the road might give us infantile paralysis but no one ever worried about cars hitting us. Anybody driving up that hill lived there and we knew when they were coming or going.

Clint lived clear over on the river side of the Court House Hill, almost in the lower end of town, but the river never got up to their house. His mother worked in my grandpa's store and my grandpa said she was a hard-working little woman. He liked her. I guess everybody liked her and Clint, too. They were quiet people but steadfast, my grandpa said.

When Clint started taking Nada Jo over to the drugstore for a coke on Saturday night and walking her home from school and from Baptist Young People's Union (we called it BYPU and thought it a little funny) on Sunday nights everybody thought it was a nice thing. Sometimes I would walk with them and keep them laughing with stories about our teachers or old Mr. Adkins that I heard my sister or Dad tell. I knew I could tell funny stories even better than Dad could.

One day when I had been telling about Miss Hazel climbing in the window of her car because the doors were so rusted they wouldn't open, Nada Jo said, "Hayes, what would we do without you? You can make people laugh no matter what happens!" I looked at Clint and he was laughing and agreeing with her. "I hope I always can, Nada Jo," I said. "War is coming."

"Don't say that, Hayes, saying it might make it happen." She took Clint's hand.

"It doesn't matter what we say, Nada Jo," Clint said, walking slowly up the steep road, kicking loose rocks in the offhand way he had, like it didn't matter whether anyone heard him or not. But people always did. "Hayes's grandpa told my mama it would probably start in the Philippine Islands."

"The Philippine Islands! Why would he say that?" Nada Jo looked at Clint.

"You tell her, Hayes, you've heard your grandpa, too.

"Well," I didn't want to upset Nada Jo, "well, Grandpa is just guessing, of course."

"What did he say, Hayes?" Nada Jo looked me straight in the eye and it was like we were playing hide-and-seek in the spyrea bushes and I'd point to where people were hiding when she was *it*. She never had to be *it* more than once. Of course I didn't care if I was *it*. Hide-and-seek was a game. War is a game, too, I thought, and I'll play any part to help her.

"Grandpa says we gave up fighting the Japanese in China so we'll have to fight them somewhere else. Of course, he means on top of fighting the Germans. Everyone knows we'll have to teach Hitler a lesson."

"Killing people doesn't teach any good lessons!" Nada Jo stepped in front of us and, being farther up the hill, her eyes were nearly level with Clint's. She would have had to look up at me, but she didn't. "I'm going to walk on home by myself." She turned and almost ran away from us up the hill toward home.

Clint and I stood staring after her for a while and then he said, "I need your help, Hayes."

"How's that, Clint?"

"I'm enlisting in the Marines as soon as I graduate and I can't tell Nada Jo."

"Why are you doing it if you can't tell her?"

"I have to, Hayes, if I don't I'll be a foot soldier. I want to be a Marine."

"I'm waiting to see what happens."

"You're smart, Hayes, you'll go to college. You might even graduate before you have to go."

"No, Clint, I won't do that. College takes money and, anyway, I want to do my part."

"Will you help me, Hayes? Will you tell Nada Jo?"

"Clint, you ought to tell her yourself. She wants to hear things from you." He would never know how it hurt to give voice to those words. I could joke and work around my feelings but not my words. "You can do it. You could always do anything that really needed doing." He was my friend. I had to say what was true.

"You're right, Hayes, just like always. You're right. Thanks." He hit my arm with his fist and started down to the gym. I went around the ridge home.

I don't know how he told her, but he did. After he left for Parris Island she started working in Grandpa's store. Grandpa said she learned faster than anybody he ever saw except his grandson, Hayes. Then he looked at me and winked.

Sometimes I walked up the hill with Nada Jo but she didn't have any books for me to carry anymore. I drove down to Huntington every Monday morning and back on Friday nights. Stayed in a boardinghouse on Third Avenue during the week. Never ate so much steak and gravy and mashed potatoes in my life. I don't think Mrs. Cleveland knew what greens were. But she helped me find my way at Marshall College. After Pearl Harbor she kept telling me to try and finish college before I enlisted. I said Uncle Sam would decide that.

Turned out that, in a way, Clint decided. He was captured at a place called Bataan, pretty much like Grandpa predicted, people said at the post office waiting for the evening mail. Nada Jo seemed to sink into herself and even I couldn't get her to smile.

One Sunday I walked up the hill with her after church and told her I was joining the army.

"Hayes, do you have to?" She looked up at me, tears starting in her eyes.

"Don't cry, Nada Jo, I'll be all right. I'll come back." Why was I telling her that, what difference did it make?

"Yes, Hayes, I think you will. I will pray for you as hard as I can." She put her hand over mine. I took it in both of my hands and it seemed to me that I had lived all my life for that one minute. "Well, I have to get home and write to Clint."

I stared at her. "Write to Clint? Nada Jo, you don't know where he is."

"I send the letters to the Red Cross and they keep trying to get them to prisoners of war."

"But, Nada Jo, Clint was in the Bataan Death March—"

"Don't you say that, Hayes, don't you dare say that. I don't ever want to hear you say that again." She was crying and almost screaming there halfway up the hill. I just stood there watching until she ran up the steps to her front door and went in, slamming the door, without looking back at me.

A lot of doors slammed that fall. Being in the army wasn't as heroic as I thought it would be. When they found out I could read fast and remember what I read they made me an instructor and sent me to Texas. Grandpa wrote that Nada Jo was still working but she was so quiet and thin he thought she'd blow away in a wind. Then, one day, I got a letter from Mother telling me Clint's mother had heard from the Red Cross. Clint was declared officially dead. It was that day that one of my students accidentally set off a grenade and I turned so a piece of metal caught me in the eye.

I told Grandpa that being treated like a hero after that was pretty embarrassing. "Don't be stubborn," he said. "People need a war hero to have dinners for and you did what you had to do."

Well, they had a dinner in my honor at the Baptist Church after which Preacher Parsons prayed for all the boys away from us and then asked me to speak. I couldn't do anything but say I agreed with his prayer. We were so hard up for laughing that people even smiled at that. I said I must have outgrown telling stories but when I looked around at their faces I couldn't disappoint them. I cleared my throat and looked extra solemn and began a story about the man who kept thinning down the paint he used in order to save money for himself. One time he painted the Baptist Church. When a big thunderstorm came and the rain washed the paint off of the church a voice out of the thunder called to him, "Repaint and thin no more!"

"You really are a wonderful person," Nada Jo said as we walked home afterward. "You can make even me feel a little bit alive."

"I'm glad, Nada Jo, you have had a sad time."

"You have had a hard time, too, Hayes. Losing one of your eyes was not easy." It seemed to me, in that moment, that it was no loss at all.

Nada Jo didn't love me the way I loved her. I knew that. But I made her see that there was a life to live and we gave the town a reason to celebrate. I don't know where people got sugar for that wedding cake but the Baptist women figured out how to make punch without using their sugar stamps. They had the drugstore get pink sherbet and they put spoonfuls of it in a big bowl of ginger ale. That sure was good.

In fact, everything was good. Nada Jo and I had an apartment over Grandpa's store and I passed exams to work for the post office. When Lily was born I thought my mother would die of pride in her namesake but it was the change in Nada Jo that made my joy complete. She quit her job in the store before the baby was born and made little clothes and fixed up a room for the crib. I had given her life and someday she would love me, of that I was sure.

But how could I guess what war and its madness would do? First there was The Bomb and then Clint's mother came down to the post office and said she had to tell me something. We walked out behind the post office and stood under a grape arbor I had built. Nada Jo loved Concord grapes.

"I have had news," she said. I looked at her eyes. They were like Clint's.

"Yes, I know, I'm sorry."

"I don't mean that, Hayes. Clint is alive. They have found him in a prisoner of war camp in Japan. I don't know what they have done to him but he is alive." She started to shake and sob and I put my arms around her till she could talk again. "You are his best friend, Hayes, and I think Nada Jo ought to know. I mean, she—" Her eyes were pleading with me.

"It's all right, I'll tell her. Don't worry."

"Bless you, Hayes, bless you." She walked around the outside of the building and I went in and finished putting up the evening mail.

When I got home Nada Jo had Lily in her high chair. She was feeding herself now and we laughed a lot at the messes she made. Nada Jo looked at me and the smile left her face.

"What is it, Hayes?" She stood stiff, in the middle of everything, like a movie picture when the film stops feeding.

"Clint is alive. He was found in a prison camp in Japan. They don't know about his condition but he's alive."

She kept standing there and all the color left her face. The baby stopped jabbering and started to cry. I took her out of her chair and washed her hands and face and took her into her room and got her ready for bed. I didn't hear a sound from the kitchen so I sang to Lily and put her in her crib.

When I went back in the kitchen Nada Jo stood with her back to me looking out the window toward the hill. The sun had just set and last light made the hill seem sharp and big.

"Do I need to tell you what I must do, Hayes?"

"No," I said like a man speaking his own death sentence.

"I am going to see Clint's mother and find out when his ship is landing. Your mother will help you with Lily."

"Will you be back for her?" I wasn't sure I had spoken out loud but I guess I did.

"No, the least I can do is let you have Lily."

"All right, Nada Jo." I went into Lily's room and took the baby in my arms long after Nada Jo had gone.

Next day I went up to Jake Hatfield's law office, but Nada Jo had been there before me. When I told him I was deserting Nada Jo and taking Lily and going to my mother's house to live and she could divorce me for desertion, Jake said to calm down. I said if he couldn't take care of it I would go to Huntington and find a lawyer.

"Nada Jo was so upset I told her to wait. But she said she would write to me and just left." Jake looked old to me all of a sudden. "But I will take care of it the way you say, Hayes." He got papers ready and I signed them.

Nada Jo left for San Francisco in two weeks, as soon as she knew when Clint was coming. I never saw them again but Lily goes to visit them in Charleston every summer. She says I should go with her. They are so good to her, she says, and they think so much of me. I tell her I know that but she is all I need in this world. She laughs at that, such a little person, and says she loves me and Grandpa and Grandma and then she tells me a funny story.

I pray she will find a good man to love because she will love him for all of her life.

Nada Jo

I always felt like I was Mrs. Fry's daughter. I can't explain it and I would never tell Mama. Maybe Mama and Mrs. Fry knew that I needed both of them. Anyway, I always knew I was not Mr. Linkus's child. He said he was my stepfather and I always called him Mr. Linkus. He was nice to me but he wasn't home much. One time I heard him and Mama quarreling and he yelled, "You don't know yourself who she is!" Mama was crying. Somehow, I knew it was my fault.

Sometimes I would take care of the Frys' little girl, Nelle. Hayes's mother and Mrs. Fry would work on quilts or make jam for the Baptist Church sales and they would let me help. They never talked much but you could tell they were real friends. Hayes called me Nelle's doll-sister so I guess his mother thought of me that way.

When Mr. Fry was alive there was so much laughing at their house it was fun just to walk by. "Look at little Jo," he would say to Mrs. Fry, "did you ever see anything so pretty?" Mrs. Fry would smile and agree and Nelle would run to me to be picked up.

Mama would send me out to the Frys' to get plums that were yellow pink. Almost like apricots, Mrs. Fry said. All of us had Mrs. Fry for our fifth-grade teacher and she never forgot any of us. But I knew I was special. She would look at me so that it made me run to her when I was little and throw my arms around her and she would put her hand on my head.

Brad Fry was only twenty-nine when he was killed at the new gas well. No one really knew in those days how to dress tools or drill but he was quick to figure things out. Having your father killed when he is only twenty-nine years old is hard but it was double hard for Nelle because everybody loved him so much. People said he was a fine carpenter and that his daddy taught him to grow the best fruit in the county. Everyone looked forward to Mrs. Fry's applesauce and sour apple cobbler when the first Early Transparents came in. The tree was beautiful in early spring and it always made me think of him. It must have been the same for Mrs. Fry. Maybe that's why she understood me so well.

Hayes was the funniest person I ever knew except for Mr. Fry. He could tell a story any time one was needed to get everybody together, but he never hurt anybody with his jokes. He was a big awkward kind man and any girl would have been lucky to get him. But most of all, for me, he was Clint's best friend.

Clint was in our grade at school but he didn't go to our Sunday School so I didn't know him until first grade. After that I always knew he was there and by eighth grade people were teasing us. My mother told me one time that Clint reminded her of someone she couldn't quite remember.

Hayes would walk up the hill with us after school and turn off around the hill just below where Mother and I lived in Mr. Linkus's house. The first time Clint held my hand was after we said good-bye to Hayes and Clint gave me his basketball ring to wear on a chain around my neck. He played guard on our high school team and they were regional champions. The team went to Logan for the tournament and I got to go and be cheerleader. Hayes's family drove up there and took me along. Clint had to ride in the bus with the team.

It was fun to be with Hayes's family, especially his grandpa. He knew so much about politics and history it was a wonder just to hear him. Hayes said he read all the time sitting down at his store. I used to borrow books from him. So did a lot of other people. He had more books than anyone.

Sometimes I wonder what would have happened if the war hadn't started. I guess Clint and I would have gotten married right after high school and Hayes would have gone to college. Maybe he would have come back and taught our children. But the war did come and, as my mother said, "We do what we have to do, what else is there?"

When Clint was taken prisoner at Bataan I went out to see Mrs. Fry and we just sat, not talking, for a long time out on the porch looking out at the Early Transparent tree. I told her I would go on working at Hayes's grandpa's store. She said that was the right thing to do.

I don't remember much about that time but I do know when I began to notice again what was going on around me. Hayes came back with the terrible injury that took one of his eyes. I was so sorry for him I would cry every time I saw him. But Hayes is Hayes and he cheered me up when I should have cheered him. I owe him so much. So much.

After I heard that Clint was declared dead I knew I would have to go on living and Hayes showed me the way to do it. Life wasn't what I had dreamed it would be but it was good. The first time I saw Hayes with our baby everything changed for me. I knew I loved him. Not like a brother or a friend, but truly, until my heart felt like it would burst. Hayes's grandpa told me that he was leaving his store to us and I could run it if I wanted to after Lily was in school. I had a real family around me, not a family partly of ghosts but a real one, and Lily would have that family all of her life.

When Hayes walked into the kitchen that evening, just when I was feeding Lily her beets and she was laughing, I knew. I looked at him and his eyes were stricken and I knew. Had I always known? I think now that I had. Clint had been declared dead but not by me. I had never felt his dying. I had patched over everything. I had hidden from myself. Maybe Hayes had done the same.

He said he knew what I had to do. We didn't have to talk. We had known each other all our lives and we both loved Clint. I had to leave Lily. I would not deny her real people to love and to be loved by. What would Clint be like? Would I ever be happy again? I didn't know. I only knew Clint would need me.

He was so thin and he moved so slowly I didn't know him at first when I saw him standing alone on the pier in San Francisco. He was staring at me, his eyes bright like the eyes of fever. I went up to him and put my arms around him and held him while he sobbed and sobbed. We would be married after he reported back to the veteran's hospital. He had to stay for six weeks of checking because he had malaria and all his ribs had been broken from being kicked.

His hair was thin and there were terrible sores on his head. Worst of all, his brave heart was tired.

He got disability pay and we got married and settled in Charleston. That is only sixty miles from Lily but there were some high mountains between us. I worked in Woodward and Lothrop's Department Store. Before long I was a buyer of housewares and china and Clint got a part-time job in the accounting department. In no time everybody there loved him. People felt grateful to all the veterans, especially the prisoners of war, but Clint was so gentle and considerate that people loved him for himself.

After Lily was old enough to understand, Hayes explained who we were and she would come and visit us. She told me all about the people at the Baptist Church and about how she called Miss Nelle Fry Aunt Nelle because she helped her so much with her studies. She said she thought Aunt Nelle wanted to marry her daddy but he said Lily was all he needed. Clint put his arms around her and said he knew that was true. I stayed awake that night long after Clint and Lily were asleep and I cried. I cried for so many people and for so many loves until I began to think about Mrs. Fry.

I imagined sitting on the porch with her when the Early Transparent was blooming and I understood at last. People live even with broken hearts. It is empty hearts that kill people, not broken ones.

Growing Up in the Navy

Paul was not likely to admit it to his mother and Luke, his kid brother, but going off to war and leaving Gassaway was scary. He would be in New York by breakfast tomorrow. The train was carrying him farther from his valley than he had ever been.

On the other hand, he was going to be a naval officer and he was already an engineer. No one made better grades than he had at West Virginia Tech and he was headed for officer training at Ft. Schuyler, New York. He sat up straighter and watched out the train window as they climbed toward Hawk's Nest.

He must have been napping when the lady in a navy suit and pink ruffled blouse spoke to him. He struggled to his feet and almost rubbed his eyes but she laughed and said, "Now you sit right back down, young man. There is a war on and we civilians should not disturb the rest of our fighting men."

"How did you know I was going to the navy?" he wondered.

"Why, you have regulation shoes and socks already and I don't know what else." She laughed in a soft, not motherly way. Maybe auntly.

As if she had read his mind she turned the next seat back so it faced him. "There are three of us and I hope you don't mind us joining you." Then he saw the smiling girls at her side. They let him put their hatboxes in the overhead bin before they settled, the aunt and one niece facing him and Lettie, the other niece, by his side. He had never smelled anything like their perfume. It was like some warm and fragrant place that he had read about.

"Where are you going, mam?" he asked.

"Well, first up to Boston then back to New Orleans. I had to go through Clifton Forge to pick up Lettie." Lettie smiled at him and he saw a gold tooth at the corner of her smile.

As darkness settled Mrs. Aubert opened a bag she carried and took out sandwiches and grapes. "This is the best Clifton Forge afforded. Please join us." She handed him a tiny linen napkin with lace on the corner. He wasn't sure where to put it. He didn't want to drop it onto the dirty train floor. He decided to tuck it into his pocket and take it out when he finished eating. "Don't you sneak off with my napkin!" Mrs. Aubert laughed. Lettie smiled at him and said they could raise the armrest between them and have a sort of table. It was like a picnic.

The time flew by for Paul, especially when Lettie's head dropped to his shoulder. He sat very still and vowed he would stay awake and not bother her, but the next thing he knew it was morning and everyone was going to the washrooms.

"I'm getting off in New York," he told them as they drank coffee bought from the conductor. "I'll be getting my training and then be assigned to a ship. I'm an engineer so they'll probably make me a cook or something."

"That is so funny," Alene, the red-headed niece laughed. "I know a man who is a chef and the army put him in charge of tending horses in the cavalry. But that was in World War I. This war is different, I expect. We will be hoping you are safe."

"Thank you," Paul stammered, aware of the blue-eyed blond girl at his side. "It would be nice if you remember me."

"We certainly will," Mrs. Aubert said, "and if you are ever in New Orleans and need a place to stay you just call us." She handed him a card with her name and New Orleans address and phone number. It was, he thought, decorative for a lady but no lady he knew had any cards at all.

They got off the train with him in New York to wait for their Boston connection. "When we get Fannie and a few things we need in Boston we will head right back to the warm weather. Don't you forget to come and see us in New Orleans." While her aunt talked Lettie smiled and waved to him. He tried to walk with dignity toward the taxi stand but he knew he was never going to walk fast and sure like the New Yorkers around him.

Ft. Schuyler was tough but he found out that he could learn as fast as any of the others in his class. Some of them were wealthy and had sailed on yachts but none of them understood how things worked better than he did. When it was time to graduate he was told that he would be going to Princeton for more training in the new field, radar. Well, I'll ship out after that, he thought, but it was on to MIT and further training before he was sent to Casco Bay, Maine, to board his destroyer escort as radar officer.

They had a few North Atlantic runs that he would just as soon forget as the war in Europe and the Pacific dragged on. When he was given orders to Houston he knew what was coming. His train arrived in New Orleans at ten at night and there was not a hotel room to be found. His train for Houston left at eight the next morning. He remembered Mrs. Aubert and thought he would like for Lettie to see him in his blues as he dug the card out of his billfold. Mrs. Aubert said on the phone to, of course, come right out, they would just love to see him, and they would have some good Creole food for him when he got there. He didn't get many words in but was soon in a taxi and on his way.

"Making the most of your time off, Mister?" the driver asked.

"I guess so," Paul yawned as he answered. At the house, which hugged the street with a balcony upstairs, he paid the driver. "How about me taking your bag in for you?" the driver winked. "No, thanks, it's not heavy," Paul answered. The driver laughed. "You'll wake up, pal."

When he went into the front room he thought he had never seen so many girls. They were everywhere, some sitting on men's laps. "Paul, honey," Mrs. Aubert greeted him, "you come right back to the kitchen and get your supper. Lettie will help you."

The kitchen was large and old-fashioned looking and Lettie had two places set close together on one side of a big worktable. "Hello, Paul," she said and smiled before she began filling bowls with delicious-smelling red soup with vegetables he had never tasted before. "We can't get much meat because of the war," Lettie said, "but we don't use much meat anyway."

"This is so good," Paul said, buttering hot crisp bread right from the oven. "Thank you, Lettie." They talked about how he liked being on a ship but he couldn't tell her about radar and how his ship would be sent out to head off the suicide planes from Japan. "My work is secret," he explained.

Her eyes widened. "Oh, Paul, you are going to Houston to be on a radar picket ship." Tears welled up in her eyes. "You are going out in front with those awful Kamikaze planes coming at you. Men talk to us here."

"I expect you are right." Paul tried to sound calm. He understood now where he was and who she was. He took her hand.

"Paul, I am going to pray every night that the war will end and that you won't go out there and get killed."

"Thank you, Lettie, and now I need some sleep."

She led him to a small room with a single bed at the

back of the house. "You rest here, Paul, and I'll have some coffee for you in the morning. And you remember my prayers, do you hear?" He nodded.

It was strange but when the news came over the radio about Hiroshima his first thought was of Lettie's prayers. They had been answered. He had expected to ship out the next day.

Lettie's prayers and the atomic bomb would always be mixed up in his mind with the way things were never quite wholly right or wrong. He had not been told about that in Gassaway.

Sweet Shrub

The smell of sweet shrub was in our house even in the winter. In the summer, it filled the air that blew through the front door straight to the back door. We had windows exactly opposite each other and Mother said Daddy had built the house for keeping cool. In the winter dried petals were in drawers and on shelves and sometimes Mason jars of rainwater had sweet shrub petals floating in them ready to rinse my hair. Mother said Daddy liked the smell, said it smelled like someplace else.

I couldn't remember him but everyone said Daddy had thought I was the prettiest child he had ever seen and he had a picture of Mother and me in his pocket when he died in the mine in Logan County.

That was part of why Alma Ruth and I got into a quarrel about Eisenhower. She said I could not vote for him because I was a birthright Democrat. I said Eisenhower *was* a Democrat.

"That is not so, Ruby Louise, he is running on the Republican ticket."

"Why do you think that is, Alma Ruth? Nobody knew

what he was till he got back from Europe and by that time everybody knew the next president would be a Republican. So he was a Republican. That doesn't make him Robert Taft." I spoke with the authority of one who is quoting word for word what she heard on the radio but I didn't tell Alma Ruth that.

"You are trying to get me off the subject. The subject is the mines and no Republican ever helped the miners, not your daddy and not mine."

"They weren't really miners, Alma Ruth, they just went up to Logan to earn some extra money to tide their families over the hard times."

"I know that but they died up there just as if they had been miners all their lives and none of the politicians till Roosevelt even knew they were there." I didn't point out they were both dead before the first Roosevelt administration because she was getting to me. She had a point.

"You have to remember, Alma Ruth, Eisenhower got us through the war. He ought to be able to get us through peace without even trying."

"Without trying, you are right about that, Ruby Louise, dead right." I was, too, as it turned out. Nothing he ever did had anything to do with us. Seemed like he mostly played golf and cooked bar-b-que, neither of which we ever tried.

But the sweet shrub bush went right ahead perfuming the air and I went right on being handy wherever I could. Aunt Addie got weakened and short of breath so I stayed with her nights for eight months before she started to mend. Nobody could tell how she got better. Sometimes after she was in bed I'd take the path around the hill and sit on the rocks and look at the valley and wonder what it would be like to be somewhere else. Not Akron, I knew about that and it was not a sweet shrub place. Gethsemene, maybe, or Bataan.

After Junior left for the Marines I went to Dr. Kessler and told him maybe I'd like to go somewhere and do war work. He said they were making war materials in Akron. I said I thought that would be fine.

Mrs. Kessler knew some people I could stay with in Akron, so I took the train from Huntington to the dirtiest place I had ever seen. There was dirt in the air and on the streets. But there were good people there. Strange, but good. Alma Ruth wrote every week and told me about who was dying, finally about Junior and that broke my heart.

Anyway, I came back and did what I could for the war in Hamlin. Mostly I ironed and cleaned for people and took care of the Kesslers' little baby. She would come to me instead of Mrs. Kessler but the poor woman was so sickly she didn't care. Hard to figure why a dentist's wife would have headaches all the time.

"Lucille Jean is a lucky little girl to have you, Ruby Louise, her mother sure can't keep up with her," Alma Ruth told me one day.

"I'm lucky, too, Alma Ruth. What would I do without that baby?"

I thought about that sometimes while Aunt Addie was sleeping, and about politics and governments and war and peace and then I'd go back to my house and put the cat out for the night. I slept on the couch in Aunt Addie's front room that smelled of sweet shrub and night-blooming cereus.

Next day I'd make a blackberry cobbler because it was little Lucille Jean's favorite. Except on her birthday. Then she had one of Alma Ruth's dried fruit cakes. Nothing else would do. I asked Alma Ruth for that recipe but she said she would make me a cake any time I wanted one. Couldn't argue with that. Actually, I did, but I didn't win.

※

"Well, Ruby Louise, what did you do for Lucille Jean Kessler this time? Mrs. Kessler said you made her act like she had some sense. She wonders how you do it."

"Alma Ruth, I just listen to the girl. Come on in the house. No use to talk out here in the heat."

"Personally, I would be hard put to listen to a girl that didn't appreciate anything that was done for her. She is drunk on her own importance. I feel really sorry when I remember how I worried my poor old mother. She couldn't get a word in for years with me talking about myself all the time."

"Lord knows how we ever grow up, Alma Ruth, who can tell anything? I just keep holding fast to the idea that the Lord *does* know."

"I know it, Lordy, I know it. Well, I've got to get on down to Lovejoy's. Rene is setting up a quilt and she can't do it by herself anymore."

After she was gone I sat in the shade on the porch

swing for a long time just smelling the lilacs and thinking about Lucille Jean. Mrs. Kessler paid me to watch Lucille Jean and I could use the money. The baby would cry and cry until I held her real tight to me and walked around sort of singing, cooing maybe. Then she would rest and go to sleep.

Years later, when she would be upset from fighting with her mother or having trouble with her friends, she would come over and I would hold her and make that noise nobody else could understand. Then I'd wash her face and tell her she ought to wear pleated skirts more because they showed her nice flat stomach or something like that and then we'd get to laughing and she'd help me for a while stringing beans or hemming somebody's curtains.

Yesterday we were sitting out on the backporch steps and I said, "Now, you listen to me, sweet child. You are worrying Mrs. Kessler to her grave and that won't do you one bit of good. You are big like me, not tiny like her, but you have been spared carrot-colored hair. Still, I can understand why you don't want red velvet to wear. I'll talk to your mother; maybe I can make up the red velvet for her and find a green plaid wool for you."

"Thank you," she whispered and started down the road to Kesslers'. That must be when Alma Ruth saw her and Alma Ruth always knows when something is right.

The sweet shrub bush by the porch was the one my mother gathered from and I always dried the flowers and made little bags of them for Lucille Jean and Alma Ruth.

One time the governor's wife came through looking for "native craft." She saw my sweet shrub drying and wanted me to make it up so they could sell it at the state cultural center. I thanked her but I never sent any to Charleston. It was Mother's bush and mine to hand on.

Miss Carrollene Tells a Story

He came up from Georgia Tech to visit with me in my trailer and he looked at me out of eyes blue like a sky sunny at noon. I saw Marmet again.

After he left I sat where I was at the table until it got dark outside. I should have been cleaning out the trailer but I was wrestling with the truth. Schoolteachers like me think a lot about the mountain children we have known, even after we retire and live in trailers. That's all there is to it. And seeing that they understand the truth is part of any teacher's job. But what was Marmet's truth?

When Marmet McCorkle told her dad, Hamilton, that she was going to marry Jack Daw Ramage and go up in the high mountains clear across McCorkle County from Linville, he said, "If you do, don't you ever come to me for help." Marmet told me she never had. Didn't need to tell me. I wouldn't have either.

Teaching as long as I have at the high school I know which children grow up truthful. I also know which ones know how much of a treasure a good story is and want to share it. My own daddy said to me more than forty years ago, "Carrollene, don't you ever be careless with stories. They need solid truth coated with a lot of fun and some tears." I never forgot that and I taught my students geometry that I kept true but coated with some puzzling. Some students got just the solid truth but Marmet learned both.

She loved Jack Daw Ramage partly because he always had time to fun. First thing he told her, when she slipped away from her daddy and went down to the roadhouse and saw the slim brown-haired Jack Daw, was "I had to get into the auto works business with a name like Ramage. You couldn't call a grocery store Ramage, could you?" She said he grinned at her and then looked serious like he was seeing something deep that was forever. I believed her. Whatever it cost, this would be the father of her children. I understood that.

The night they ran away they took the train to Nashville and stayed at the hotel down near the Opry. She didn't ask how he could afford it. Already she knew he was like that.

They lived up over the auto works and garage out on the gravel road that went up the mountain. The garage smell was on everything but when Jack Daw came up the outside back steps he cleaned his feet and went straight to the back room to take off his oily clothes. Marmet would take him a pan of hot water. They didn't have indoor plumbing there for four years, the year their baby boy was born, Young Jack. Their first baby, a little girl, died when she was just two days old. Marmet's ma told me Marmet didn't have any care. Don't know how she knew, she never went up on the mountain.

One time when I was at their house, I saw Jack Daw kiss Marmet gingerly on the cheek on his way to the back room. When he was clean he grabbed her around the waist and danced her around the kitchen, both of them laughing like children. She bought the strongest detergent she could find and took their clothes to the launderette at the crossroads but things still smelled. I think that was all right with her.

Ma and Pa Ramage lived up on the mountain above where the gravel road ends. Ma told Marmet to sweep but not stir the dust up. Ma laughed a lot and the family followed her around, settling in whatever room she was cooking or sewing or ironing in. She liked the old ballad about the woman who fought dirt all her life and then was buried in dirt. "They will bury me in dirt," I heard her say, "but I don't ever aim to fight it!"

Jack Daw's daddy would laugh at her jokes when he was sober and stay away when he wasn't. He would sit reading books all evening, books he taught Jack Daw to read. Marmet thought that was about the luckiest combination of pa and ma a man could have. She tried to be like her mother-in-law, to let a lot of things be.

When people from Florida began coming up into the mountains for the summer, Jack Daw's business began to grow. Marmet got the idea of renting cars to the retired people who began to stay all year. She fixed the space up over the garage for an office and they built the house halfway up when young Jack was twelve.

I know she had to find some money for the rental

business but she never asked Hamilton McCorkle. Russell Kingery over at the bank always had been struck on Marmet, and I went over to the bank and told him about the business. He said that would be a fine investment and he went up and talked to Marmet. Through the years he was up there a lot, especially after Jack Daw began to drink and Marmet needed help. But the trust for Jack's college wasn't from him. Hamilton McCorkle set that up. He was proud of his grandson and he would have helped Marmet if she had asked. They were a lot alike, those two.

I tried to get her to talk to her daddy once about how teachers weren't paid a fair wage. She agreed that as president of the school board for twenty years, he ought to do something about that. But she couldn't bring herself to talk to him, even to help me and the other teachers. I don't know why I didn't talk to him.

The Holiness Church of Deliverance got started over at the Skyline Shopping Center and Manda McCorkle got caught up in that stuff all the way. None of us said much to the McCorkles after that.

Ma Ramage told young Jack there is more than one way to be a good man. He knew and I knew that Marmet would never leave Jack Daw even when she had lots of chances. The truth is she was a one-man woman. I understand that. The cancer that killed her may have been made worse by gasoline fumes, who knows? But it was not caused by Jack Daw. He stayed away when he was drunk just like his daddy did before him and he loved Marmet till the day she died.

"Am I like my daddy?"

"Well, you certainly have the engineer's mechanical understanding," I hedged.

"My mother was more like you than she was like Grandma McCorkle, wasn't she?"

"Well, teachers have a lot of influence."

"They sure do. Wouldn't like to go with me over to see Grandpa McCorkle, would you?"

"No, thanks, not today."

He turned at the door. "She even had wavy hair like you."

I nodded, not trusting all truth to words.

The Fellowship at Wysong's Clearing

"Well, Ruby Louise, it has happened. I knew it would. It was just a matter of which out-of-the-way place it would be. A bunch of hippies has moved in up at Wysong's Clearing."

"Good heavens, are you sure? There isn't any house up there."

"They went over to West Hamlin to Waggoner's Lumberyard and bought a bunch of stuff to build lean-tos to live in while they make bricks out of the clay around Adkins's pigpen!"

"I never heard of such a thing. I'd like to see how they do that."

"You're as bad as Old Man Adkins. He just let them come in over his land back around on the other side of the hill and take their jeep right up to Wysong's Clearing. They are dirty and they are strange."

"Well, they don't have a corner on dirty and strange around here, Alma Ruth, but I do wonder who sold them that land. I never thought about it belonging to anybody."

"Maybe nobody did, Ruby Louise, maybe they're on public land and John Mayhew can make them leave. We have public school picnics up there, after all. I am going down and talk to John Mayhew at the bank and tell him we don't need filthy people living up there without the benefit of marriage. Are you coming with me?"

"I don't think so, Alma Ruth. I've been having a hard time getting rid of this cough." Which was not quite the reason but it served.

"You ought to make some steam and put Mentholatum in the water and breathe the fumes. There's no use for you to fool around what with your mama dying of TB, Ruby Louise."

"You're right, Alma Ruth. I'll take care."

"I'll bring your mail on the way back so you can just stay in today."

"Thanks, Alma Ruth, I'm obliged to you."

After she left I got to thinking about young couples starting out new up there on that hill where you could see all across the valley to the covered bridge. It got me to thinking about my fiancé, Junior, killed so long ago at Bataan, and suddenly I was crying like I hadn't cried since the war. It seemed like I couldn't stop but I finally fell asleep in the rocking chair in the kitchen where I usually sew while I'm watching the cooking. I was nodding there when someone practically knocked the back door down.

I stumbled to my feet and yelled, "I'm not deaf. Wait a minute."

When I opened the door, I just stood there and looked. I had to take it all in. Her hair just hung. It was halfway down her back and she had a band around her forehead keeping it out of her eyes. Her skirt was made of old overall material and it hung almost to the ground. And she had on boots. Not overshoes, boots.

Don't know how long I stood there like a fool, but it was long enough to give her the advantage if she had wanted to take it. But she didn't. She just said, "Miss Ruby Louise, Aunt Addie said I ought to come and see you."

"Is Aunt Addie your aunt?"

She laughed, kind of merry sounding with her eyes squinted, and said, "No, I wish she was, but she said everyone called her that and I should, too."

"I'm a little surprised at that."

"So was I, but pleased. To tell the truth, I doubt she could see me very well." And she laughed that merry laugh again and I knew she was including herself among things to laugh at. It was then I opened the door wider and said she should come on in, what was I thinking keeping her out on the back porch.

"Thank you." She sat down at the kitchen table where I pointed.

"Now, let me get you some coffee. I was just ready myself and I have some sweet cakes."

"Oh, I want to learn how to make them for my children."

"You have children up there on top of the hill living in—" I stopped. I don't really like to be caught in gossip.

She didn't seem surprised. "Yes, I have two little girls, two and three. Hope and Charity."

At first I though she was starting to preach or beg but

then I realized she had named her little ones those old-fashioned names. "Well, those are pretty names. Uncommon, though."

"Yes, I know, but I hope they'll live up to them."

"Now, that is a fine thing, giving names to live up to. Imagine living up to Ruby Louise!"

We both laughed, and in the middle she said, "Or Jane! See Jane run!"

"Oh, oh, see Jane run. See Jane run after Spot." We laughed harder. Then I caught myself. "Is Jane your name? I'm mortified, Jane. I didn't mean to laugh at your name."

"It's all right, Miss Ruby Louise, you were laughing at yours."

"Why, that's right, Jane. Here, have some more coffee. Sweet cakes are good for children, not much sugar and you can add bran. I used to use rendered chicken fat in them but now I just get oil at the store. Don't put any cinnamon in them, that makes them taste heavy. Nutmeg is right with a little bit of lemon flavor."

"Can I watch you make them some time?" It seemed like that was a natural thing for her to ask.

"You sure can. And bring the babies. They can play here on the floor."

Suddenly I thought, *What is going on,* and it must have shown on my face because she said, "You must wonder why Aunt Addie sent me down here. Well, she said she was too old to teach me much and besides she never was that handy. But if I was going to survive up on that hill I had better find out from Ruby Louise how to do things. I really would be grateful to learn from you."

"What do you want to learn?"

"How to can and preserve berries, how to make rugs, how to get things done . . . "

"What have you learned already, Jane?"

"I went to the University of Wisconsin, Miss Ruby Louise, and I got two degrees in history. I'm a good learner," she grinned, "but maybe not very sensible, not handy like Aunt Addie says you are."

"Well, what did you learn from history?"

Well, for nearly an hour she told me about the French and all the things they tried in Indochine and how we were trying all the same things all over again with the exact same results—dead young men. I said I had never seen the sense in war, but, after all, I was a woman. She said the men in their fellowship believed like she did. Her man never registered for the draft.

"Is he a Quaker or something?" I asked.

"No, he isn't against all of anything, even war. He has to make a judgment on each one and this one he thinks is ill advised."

"But doesn't he go along with the majority—this is a democracy, isn't it?"

"He's not sure the majority wants this war. Congress never declared it. Do you want this war?"

"No, I don't, Jane. And you're right, nobody in Washington asked me." We exchanged the rueful grins that it came to me women had always exchanged. "I'll help you if I can. You bring your, er, fellowship down here Sunday for dinner and we'll plan what to do."

She looked at me and said, "I'm very happy to have met you, Miss Ruby Louise."

"Goodbye, Jane," I said. "Here, take the rest of these sweet cakes to your young ones."

Jane had just started up the hill beyond my house when Alma Ruth burst in the front door without knocking. "Ruby Louise," she yelled, "are you all right?" She was wild-eyed and red in the face.

"Of course I'm all right, Alma Ruth. What is wrong with you?"

"I saw one of those hippies leaving here when I was coming out of the post office and I ran as fast as I could."

"I'm sorry you didn't get here in time to meet Jane."

"Jane who?" I burst out laughing. "And just what is so funny?" Alma Ruth demanded.

"I don't even know what her family name is—I didn't even ask."

"And what is so funny about that?"

"Well, you'll find out in due time, Alma Ruth, when you come over for Sunday dinner."

"Thank you, Ruby Louise, I would like to come and I'll bring a dried fruit cake. But why can't you tell me about this Jane now?"

"Because all the hippies will be here and you can find out for yourself."

"What do you mean, here?"

"For Sunday dinner."

She stared at me for a while. "I might have known. Aunt Addie sent them down here to you. They have been practically camping with her, taking advantage of her being so old she can't see them. Probably can't smell them either. You would think, though, that their vulgar talk would be enough even if she can't see or smell them."

"Have you ever heard them talk, Alma Ruth?"

"No, but I don't see why I should. We don't need any strange people here."

"What do we need, Alma Ruth?" I felt anger I didn't know was in me and my voice shook. She stared.

"There is something going on here. Why are you being nice to these strangers, Ruby Louise?"

Because, I thought, what if I had spoken up against the other war, like Jane and her fellowship were doing with this war? What if Bataan hadn't happened, and Junior hadn't been killed? What if—I was crying till I couldn't talk.

Alma Ruth stumbled over and put her arms around me. "Don't cry, Ruby Louise. I'll bring two dried fruit cakes. Those children work hard and they'll be hungry. And I'll tell them how to make chow-chow out of those green tomatoes. They put in tomato seeds instead of plants and didn't get any ripe. Don't cry, please, don't cry."

"You've been thinking about how they need help, haven't you?"

"Not till today, Ruby Louise. John Mayhew told me

they were homesteading that land and it was legal and we had better get used to it if we had any sense. So I guess they've got every right to be here."

Saturday morning I stewed three chickens with onions, ready to drop dumplings in after church on Sunday. The chard and turnip tops were just cold enough in the garden to taste their best. Cabbage was crisp and I still had bell peppers to cut up with it for salad. Alma Ruth's cakes were all the sweet we needed, but I felt like it was a time to celebrate so I cooked stewed apples and opened some pickled peaches.

John Mayhew walked back from church with Alma Ruth and me, like he often does, and stayed for dinner. The young people from up the hill didn't take their jeep around the back way. They just walked straight down, stretched almost across the road there were so many of them.

Jane stood on the porch with a baby in her arms and the blondest boy I ever saw stood by her, holding another little girl by the hand. The little one was peeking out of a sheep-skin hood.

"This is Olaf, Miss Ruby Louise." He held out his big hand.

"You look like a Viking," I laughed as we shook hands.

"Well, I guess I am. Kvalheim is my name. My grand-parents came from Norway."

"That is sure something new for Hamlin. You all come right in. This is Alma Ruth and Mr. John Mayhew Grass."

"How do you do, Mrs. Kvalheim." John Mayhew is always exceptionally proper and exceptionally dumb on Sundays.

"I am Jane Cohen, Mr. Grass," Jane said quietly.

"Oh, of course, I—"

"Come on in, all of you," I interrupted and told everybody to take their coats into my bedroom and put them on the bed. When they got into my room they all started exclaiming at once about the quilt on the bed. Alma Ruth got so busy telling them how she thought up the pattern I could tell she forgot they weren't married.

Sally, one of the hippie women, asked if she could help me put the food on and I said of course she could. She had the nicest way of doing things, making them look just a little bit better. I don't know what that is but I know it when I see it. Alma Ruth has it too, so I suspected the two of them would hit it off.

We all gathered around the big table in the dining room and John Mayhew gave thanks. Then you should have seen those young folks eat. I never saw anything like it. Baby Charity sat on my lap and chewed on a chicken leg bone. I tell you that felt nice to me.

John Mayhew asked Olaf if he had always been a carpenter. "No, I went to medical school, Mr. Grass, but I dropped out in my last year."

"Why did you do that?" John Mayhew was genuinely shocked.

"It seemed to me I had to find a simpler way to live. Making money isn't enough for me."

"Well, I can tell you," Alma Ruth was indignant, "you won't have to worry about a lot of money from people around here who haven't had a doctor since old Doc Ashworth died in 1939. We have to go clear over the hill to West Hamlin."

"Oh, I'm not licensed for West Virginia and, anyway, I'm busy building our house right now."

"Then you did finish learning to be a doctor?" John Mayhew never would let a thing rest.

"I want to hear about the house," I interrupted. "What's it going to be like?"

Thomas, the quiet small one, spoke up at last and his eyes gleamed as he held Sally's hand and talked about that house. "It will have all windows on the south and west to make it warm when the leaves drop in fall. I'm drying sassafras and walnut for the woodwork inside. The stairway will have carved posts all the way up and there'll be wooden shutters and kitchen cabinets."

"I'll make a quilt with a sassafras leaf design for your bed," Alma Ruth said. Then she blushed.

"We are honored, Miss Alma Ruth, but that will be art and we'll hang it on our wall for our children to see as they grow up." It came to me that this was a strange conversation but uncommonly interesting.

After dinner Thomas and Olaf said they and John Mayhew would do the dishes and we should play with the babies in the front room. Well, John Mayhew looked surprised but he went right along with the fun. For once, I had enough sense not to say anything.

The sun was going down by the time they left but I said it would still be light up on the hill. They said yes, they got the light first and lost it last.

Then John Mayhew and Alma Ruth got their coats, but it felt like something needed saying.

"This is a new day, Ruby Louise. It's going to be hard for those young people here but I hope they make it."

"Don't be so old-fashioned, John Mayhew," Alma Ruth had passed through all her doubts. "We need a doctor and someone who knows what to do with wood around here and if Aunt Addie and Ruby Louise approve of them, so do I."

Well, I'm slower than they think, I guess. There was a fear in me, a distrust of happiness on that hill. It didn't stop me, but it weighed me down.

"Those babies are so sweet," I said and Alma Ruth hugged me and John Mayhew cleared his throat and patted me on the shoulder as he went out the door.

I made myself a cup of sassafras tea and sat without the lights on for a long time after they left. Carving on sassafras, I thought, that is going to be something to see.

Crisis at Bald Knob

To see Zevelda the way she was that Sunday is, well, not something you're very likely to see. When she gets mad she runs around and squawks for all the world like a chicken you don't have a good grip on when you lay the hatchet to its neck. But this wasn't Zevelda mad. She wasn't really puzzled either, although she didn't understand how she felt. She was more hopeless, lost, and it took even me a long time to be with her in her feelings. It wasn't that I wasn't willing. I will go through the lowest valley with Zevelda. It was just that I felt somehow to blame, somehow wrong.

Now, don't misread me. I'd do it again but I can't really enjoy success, or even know where success is. There is this I have come to see, though. Roger Williams started our brand of Baptist church so the people of the church could rule themselves and include a lot of different folks. Well, the Bald Knob Baptist Church where I go is proud to be descended from Mr. Williams. However, several members do pray for his soul, late departed, because he doubted that the Baptist Church really started in the Upper Room.

Now, when you have people praying that you are going

to believe just like they do, I ask you, what chance is there for democracy to operate?

Anyway, when Althea Sponaugle's man left the same day as Roman Turley's youngest girl and neither one of them ever showed up again, Althea gave herself to the Lord and Bald Knob Church was her chosen field to harvest. She taught Sunday School, was program chairman of Ladies Aid, and the leading planner of church dinners inside of a year.

It was a wonder what she could get done but people quit showing up to see her do it. Not all at once, you understand, it was more that people began to feel peaked and stay home or went to visit kin over the hill somewhere on Sunday or on Thursday when Aid met.

"Hollene," Zevelda told me, "that woman is driving people away. Nobody wants to be bossed around."

"How can you say that, Zevelda?" People like Althea make you stall for time when you are talking about them. "Why, she does more work than anybody."

"Have you read the story of Martha and Mary lately, Hollene?" She knew she had scored. Martha was a handywoman, no doubt about it. Well, so I'm a Martha, but people don't stay away from church dinners when I make fried chicken and beans with a little bit of onion like old Miss Hettie likes and I ask Zevelda to make banana cakes. No, they do not stay away. I know that for a fact. Even the church Marys are cheerful at those dinners.

Well, last Sunday I was feeling off my food a little and didn't go to church. I kept expecting to get sicker as the morning went by but, by the time Zevelda stopped after church, I was ready to cook dinner. She took advantage, too.

"Well, I see you decided to get out of the congregational business meeting after church. Do you think John or Peter or Thomas would have missed a meeting called by Jesus?"

"Jesus didn't call meetings. Anyway, he told them what to do. He didn't ask them."

"You are making that up but, anyway, I am sorry I went."

Then I was ashamed. "Zevelda, I'm sorry. What is wrong?"

"Well, we have a new moderator, Althea Sponaugle."

I stared at Zevelda, my hands halfway to the coffeepot. She just stood there looking at me, her arms half out of her coat. I don't know how long it was before she said, "Did you hear me?"

"Yes, I heard you."

"Well?"

"Well, what?"

"What are we going to do?"

"Turn Methodist?"

"Don't be silly, Hollene. We have got to get rid of her." The time for talk was done.

Our chance came sooner than we expected. The Reverend Luther Wesley Bailey from Charleston came to give a talk at Bald Knob and we fixed a big dinner even though working with Althea took the spirit out of it. There wasn't quite as much laughing as usual and the beans had just a shade too little seasoning. Not enough to point to but you knew it.

The Reverend Bailey sat beside Althea and told stories all through dinner. One thing about having a visiting preacher, we do get a fresh supply of stories to tell the Methodists. Anyway, by the time we went up the basement steps to the meeting room to hear his message, Zevelda and I knew what we were going to do. His message was about how the state Baptist Convention needed money to keep their offices in Charleston in good working order so they would have educated, dedicated leaders to send out to speak to us.

"About giving money so they could keep their offices in Charleston in good working order so——," I whispered to Zevelda.

"Be still," she said, "we have got to bide our time."

When Reverend Bailey finished and Mrs. Lovejoy started playing "Will There Be Any Stars in Your Crown?" softly on the piano we were supposed to go forward and put a pledge in the plate and shake Reverend Bailey's hand. When Zevelda got up there she said, "Reverend Bailey, this evening has given me a whole new idea about the church and I want to hold onto the light I have been privileged to glimpse." I stopped dead in my tracks, halfway up the steps of the altar.

"Why, thank you, and God bless you," he said, shaking her hand and patting her shoulder at the same time.

"Yes sir," she said, "we need to have our very own, a

Bald Knob Christian, on the state board so we never lose sight of that light again."

"Why, that is a good idea. I'll talk to the board soon."

"There is no need to hesitate, sir." You could hear a mouse moving under the floorboards in that church. "We have, right here, the most able church woman in this state and, while we would miss her guidance, we will send her as our sister to Charleston. Althea Sponaugle's talent was never meant to serve just Bald Knob."

By this time, Mrs. Lovejoy had paused in her piano playing and Zevelda was speaking up. Althea protested, "Why, how could I ever serve at the state level?"

Then there was a mighty affirmation from the membership raised as one voice of thanksgiving for the chance to send one of their own.

Well, the Reverend Bailey put Althea to work on committees and the first thing we knew she was taking the train to Philadelphia for training meetings and polishing her fingernails. They say she eventually got into ecumenical work but by that time she had moved to Charleston.

Jake Koontz went back to ringing the church bell and taking the money to the bank. Said we could call him moderator if we wanted to but all he was going to do was ring the bell and take the money.

One time I asked Zevelda whether she was a little bit ashamed. She looked at me and said, "It was your idea."

I said, "Why, I didn't say a word." She never did believe me.

The Handywoman

My profession was decided before I was ten. People would say, "Isn't that little old Ruby Louise the handiest little thing you ever saw?" when I helped to carry out the dishes at church suppers. Years later they would say, "Get Ruby Louise. I'll declare that woman can do anything. She is that handy."

Naturally I got handier all the time and I will say that, in Hamlin, right now, there is not another woman who is as handy as I am. People who want someone with them when they're dying or grieving call on me. New slipcovers and braided rugs are my doing. I make up the berries from over beyond the graveyard hill and string beans on strings to dry so the church can have leather britches and cobbler for their dinners. Older people really like those brown beans left in their dry pods and cooked all day with pork. The young people think it is quaint.

Of course, it wasn't quaint when I learned to dry vegetables and fruit. My mother taught me because we didn't have any refrigerators and not many canning jars. That's why Alma Ruth learned to make dry fruit cake, too, but people like it just because it is so good. I never saw anyone turn down a piece with its fringe of caramel icing. I always told her I wasn't going to try to make it because her standards were too high for me. She laughed and said she liked to make them because people thought of her as the cake maker and never asked her to do anything else, most of which would have been harder.

We were friends, Alma Ruth and me, when we went to the old grade school to Miss Hettie Lucas's first grade. Miss Hettie had every child in her class reading before the year was over. She'd hold up cards and have us read what they said real fast till all of us got to laughing. Then she had us learn the alphabet and make sounds from letters. Some of us were good at one and some at the other. We built a town in a sandbox in the corner of the room that had clean roads all laid out and houses with porches and flowers in the yards. We made the flowers out of pieces of crepe paper. One time Alma Ruth made a green petunia with pink leaves and Junior Grass laughed. Miss Hettie tapped him across the back with her ruler and said that was Alma Ruth's petunia colored as she saw it. That might help to explain why Alma Ruth never did use dried apples in her cake. Apples was what everybody else used.

Sometimes I get to thinking about how we *are* kind of decides how we'll act. During the Vietnam mess Hamlin watched while the young drop-outs started a folklore school at Wysong's Clearing. Then Jane and Olaf, founders of the school, moved down off the hill and left Sally, Thomas, and Alma Ruth to enlarge the school. That seemed natural enough, but the truth is, it nearly cost Alma Ruth her sense of humor.

One day she came in the back door without knocking and didn't even answer my, "Well, good morning," before she poured herself a cup of coffee and sat down at the kitchen table.

"Take your coat off and stay a while, Alma Ruth." I knew her well enough to hazard a pretty good guess about her mood and this was unnatural and heavy. There were dark swollen circles under her eyes.

"I am going to Washington for the Peace March." She dared me to reply with every syllable.

"Well, now, that's exciting, Alma Ruth."

"Don't pretend with me. You are just like everybody else. Calling those young people hippies was bad enough —look who's wearing jeans now!—but calling them Communist is evil!"

"I don't call them Communists, Alma Ruth, I don't even call them hippies."

"You know what I mean, Ruby Louise. Linville Johnson and Elijah Fisher put an ad in the *Lincoln Republican*. Here it is!" She held out the paper, which she had just gotten in her mail.

"Lordy, that cost them a pretty good sum," I stalled.

"Money is no object to people who hate!" she shouted.

"You are right about that but only people with a lot of money can afford to be so choosy about their friends."

"Now that is a fine way to talk." It came to me it had been a dumb way to talk. "Does that mean you are not choosy? Maybe you are my friend only because you can't afford to play bridge with Emmaline Johnson."

"Alma Ruth, Emmaline Johnson still celebrates the birth of Joseph McCarthy and thinks the Northern Methodist Church started in the Upper Room. Why would I play anything with her? And you know I don't like any game where people don't talk."

It came to me we were losing our way. We were saying things that didn't need saying and being still about things that needed hearing. Alma Ruth left after a while just like she came, mad at a world that included me.

I watched the Peace March on TV but I never could pick out Alma Ruth. When she got back days passed and she didn't come to see me. I cleaned the basement and made two rugs for the nursery at church but my mind was blank and I tired easily. My body is never far behind my spirit, I notice.

But Jane came to see me. I thought she'd tell me about meeting Dr. Spock in Washington but that was not what she had come to say. "A group of people, Ruby Louise, lawyers and the Methodist preacher—"

"Which Methodist preacher—southern or northern?" I interrupted, trying to lighten things.

"You know they don't use those names anymore."

"All right, Democrat Methodist or Republican Methodist?"

"You are impossible!" She fell into a chair laughing. "Republican, of course, people with money. They have gotten a petition to get me out of the high school principal's job."

"Why, Linville Johnson hasn't had a child in school since Roosevelt was elected the second time."

"Not having children doesn't keep you from paying taxes or contributing to political campaigns, and Linville Johnson is slick about that!" Her eyes were narrowed and I thought they were as near to sparking as eyes can get. "They, Ruby Louise, are calling me a Communist!"

"Jane," I said, "sit down and let's quit trying to sound like Linville Johnson. We don't have it in us." She started to talk back but smiled as I sat down and poured coffee. Sweet cakes were under a glass cover on the table.

"Just like the first time I came to see you when I had just gotten here and was so afraid."

"Well, none of us changes much and times just seem to repeat themselves."

"What can I do?" She looked me straight in the eye and I talked straight to her.

"Well, you can quit thinking that Linville Johnson will think deep enough to change his mind. If he went more than a quarter of an inch in he would be out of raw material." She laughed, I was relieved to see.

"Next," I said, "you can leave this to me and keep Alma Ruth out of it." There was a stillness between us that quivered and then breathed deep.

"All right, I know when I'm out of my depth. I love you, Ruby Louise." I colored at that and pushed her out the door so I could start planning.

Next morning, it was a Wednesday, an action day, I waited in Linville Johnson's office while the great man talked football with Homer Fry. I was as calm as I have ever been in my life. One thing about having a plan, having your mind made up, is that it is calming, no matter how hard the plans are to carry out. And this plan was easy.

"Good morning, Miss Ruby Louise, you come right in here and sit down and tell me what I can do for you." He closed the door to the waiting room and bowed me to a chair across the big desk from him. I thought, he is one of three people in this county who still has to remind me I am unmarried by calling me Miss. The other two are also Northern Methodists.

"I won't take much of your time, Mr. Johnson," I said in a voice so proper it would have made anyone but Linville Johnson vomit. "Actually I didn't come here to have you do anything for me. I am prepared to do something for you. It has occurred to me that if Jane Kvalheim doesn't stay principal at the high school I am going to find it impossible not to report to your Emmaline what I learned cleaning out at the Widow Purdy's house. Good-bye, Mr. Johnson, and thank you for your time."

I walked right out the door, down the hill, and into my house without looking back. The last time I saw him he was sitting with his mouth open. Don't know when he closed it.

Whenever it was, he seemed to have swallowed Communist in connection with Jane for good.

Alma Ruth came over within half an hour of when I got home and said, "My cousin Icylene works in the office next to Linville Johnson and she called me as soon as she heard from his secretary what you did. You were just guessing. You haven't cleaned for the Widow Purdy for fifteen years!"

"I don't guess, Alma Ruth. I deduce. Anyway, you can always count on anyone who accuses other people of bad acting having something on his own conscience."

We hugged each other then and laughed and declared Hamlin's first Vietnam victory.

I guess we would have been friends even if our daddies hadn't both died in the mine explosion at Holden when they went up there just to make a little money and then come back home. But, also, we kind of fitted. She made things beautiful and I made them work. We thought the same about life and about death, too, how temporary they are.

Tears Need Shedding

What I remember most about being baptized in Mud River is coming out of the water. The preacher was holding my arm but he was the one who slipped in the mud on the flat rock we used for taking off and returning to the bank. I caught him and then he handed me over to Aunt Ruby and her pine tree quilt. It felt good. It was turning cold like it can in March.

But that is not what I meant to tell. As I came out of the water, full of being forgiven and possibilities, I looked up toward the roof of Sweetland's Store where three boys were watching me. Boys always watched baptisms from up there but I saw only one pair of eyes and my heart burns still from them. It is part of my salvation.

Everybody in town knew that Eddie Bill Unger's mother killed his daddy to save the life of Trooper Will McCoughlin. As it was, Trooper Will was nearly shot in the foot but that was nothing compared with what that drunken husband had done to Mrs. Unger. After the Unger family moved to town and settled in old Mrs. Pridemore's garage apartment, Miss Lavonia found out what beautiful quilting Mrs. Unger could do and helped her sell some of her work. But she still had to take in washing to keep her children in school. We thought that after a while they would talk about their sad past but they never did.

Eddie Bill was two years ahead of me in school but he was six years older than me. He didn't get much chance to go to school while Mr. Unger was alive. Miss Lavonia invited the family to the Baptist Church but they never came. I thought they were shy till that day I saw Eddie Bill on the roof of Sweetland's Store. He had salvation inside him.

Sometimes when we played Chinese checkers at our house and Grandma made taffy out of sorghum, the old-fashioned way in an iron skillet, Eddie Bill would come. It was understood, I think, that anyone Miss Lavonia approved of was invited and every kid in town had had her in the fifth grade. Anyway, Eddie Bill would come and laugh and pull taffy, sometimes with me. We would pull till it was the palest yellow Grandma said she had ever seen. Most people started eating it way before it got that light.

Daddy asked Eddie Bill if he was going to Alderson Broaddus College at Philippi. Miss Lavonia told us he had a scholarship there. Eddie Bill said no, he was going to West Virginia University and study police science and be a police-man like Trooper Will.

"Well, that's interesting, Eddie Bill," Daddy said, "Of course, Will is in law school now."

"I know that but I will stay in the force like Captain Monday has done."

"That is a high calling, Eddie Bill," Daddy said. "I hope it works for you."

"Thank you, sir," Eddie Bill sort of mumbled.

Late in his senior year Eddie Bill started going over to the drugstore on Friday nights and dancing in the back by the jukebox with Betty Lee Ray. I would go over there with my friend Junie Gillenwater and we would get my cousin Dillard to make us vanilla or lemon cokes while we pretended not to see the dancers. Once Eddie Bill asked me to come on back and dance but I said I had to go home.

Once he came to BYPU, we never called it Baptist Young People's Union, and sort of hung around in the back of the church. I could feel him there and wanted him to come on in but he didn't.

Daddy came home one evening and said it beat all the way that Unger boy fought off everybody that tried to help him. Refused a job in Grandpa's store and started hanging around Holley's Pool Hall till Old Man Holley gave him a job serving beer and cleaning the floor. "That," Daddy said, "is no way to get to Morgantown or to any other university."

Grandpa said it wasn't much wonder when you considered what that boy had been through, had to kill Crede Gillenwater to keep him off his mama.

"What do you mean, Grandpa?" I didn't believe Eddie Bill could kill anybody.

"Why, honey, he was the oldest son. He had to protect his ma."

"Where was his daddy, Grandpa?" I cried.

"Why, he was drunk, too. Drunk and fired up and probably laughing."

Daddy looked at me and said, "Honey, that was a long time ago when Eddie Bill was just a child up in the hills. We can't judge what he did."

"But you are judging him," I said and the tears that wouldn't fall were behind my eyes. My head felt like it would explode.

Grandma was hemming a complicated pleated skirt for me and only half listening. "Truth is Eddie Bill looks just like his daddy. Don't know how a mother could handle that." I went to my room but I didn't cry.

Daddy was right. Eddie Bill kept on at Holley's after graduation and I would walk along the other side of the road from the pool hall and try to get a glimpse of Eddie Bill out of the corner of my eye. One day he came out and called, "Well, howdy, Miss Lily." I looked at him and would have answered but I saw the silly smile on his face that I knew comes with being drunk. He was lost. Salvation was gone from his eyes.

I ran up the hill and went straight to my room and threw myself on my bed. Out the window the broom sage on the hillside was playing in the summer wind that came and then went.

It was a late summer day and I was returning with my family for a visit to Galloway. As we started up the long climb to the top of the West Hill, a man in old army fatigues came up over the lower side of the road. My husband stopped the car and asked if we could give him a ride. It was Eddie Bill. He looked once at me and then at my engineer husband. "No thank ye," he said and turned back down the bank toward an old frame house with a rust-streaked tin roof.

"I guess he wasn't going over the hill," my husband said and we continued on our way. Tears that held behind my eyes made my head pound as I looked out the car window at the devastated hillside of locust trees dead from the blight. In the backseat little Ella Jo said, "Poor man. Poor house."

"Yes," I said and a tear dropped onto my denim skirt.

Snap Beans and Petits Fours

Maude had been conducting a staff meeting when he called. Her secretary was visibly shocked when she came into Maude's office. "Mrs. Pridemore, a man called while you were in the meeting. Wants you to call back."

"Who was it? Did he say?"

"Said he was your husband," Marie said, stumbling over the words.

"A crank?" she asked before she thought. Truly, she had no husband. "Thank you. I'll call."

She asked Marie to close her office door and slowly walked to her desk and sat down. It seemed as though her body was refusing to act. Wisely, she almost laughed to herself.

Fresh out of Wellesley, idealistic, and, yes, poor, she had taken the private tutoring job in West Virginia. Mr. Lucas, a mine owner, offered a good salary. She wanted to make the world better for children but jobs were hard to get.

Her first impression of Logan was darkness. Almost immediately she associated it with coal dust but it would be months before she realized how short the days actually were when the valley is narrow and the hills steep and high. Roman Harmon, his long form almost folded under the steering wheel, drove her from the depot to the big Lucas house. He told her he was usually at the mines but he had a cough lately. Maude had never heard such a cough and wondered at the Lucas family exposing themselves to such an infection.

The house where she would live and work was the largest square structure she had ever seen. Red brick with a concrete porch, it was somehow dingy. Walking up the steps, she saw, for the first time, the glitter in the dust as an errant sunbeam played on it. Black gold, she thought. Mrs. Lucas opened the door and her joy at seeing Maude poured from her brimming eyes. Maude thought she was a woman who had reason to cry a lot.

They called the child Little Lonnie and little he was. Congenital heart defects prevented him from normal activity and normal growth. It was Maude who brought to the dark house the sound of singing and the magic of friends like Robinson Crusoe and Hans Brinker. The child grew in mind and spirit and, before his death three years later, his parents saw joy in his face. For this, they were forever in Maude's debt, but they were powerless to protect her when she met Cain.

She first saw the schoolteacher from Holden mining camp at a church social. He came into Logan on weekends and sometimes brought some of his older students from Holden School. He was easily the most popular man in the room wherever he found himself and he chose to eat supper with Maude. When she was asked to sing he walked with her to the piano and watched as she played and sang, her fingers limber and slim, her voice sweet and high. He proudly walked her home later. Someday he would go to college as she had, he told her, and then he would be a proper teacher.

Mrs. Lucas warned Maude about life in Holden but Maude was in love and World War I had begun. Cain enlisted and came home on leave to tell her he was going to Puerto Rico and he could take a wife. They were married by a justice of the peace in Logan and the Lucas family gave them a clock and a hundred dollars.

Maude's mother sent a tear-stained letter of love and worry from Massachusetts. Maude knew it was not the war that her mother feared. It was West Virginia.

They lived in the old fort in San Juan. It was crude and damp and romantic. Soldiers marching so far from Argonne seemed like wonderfully dressed and exciting actors in a play under sun and moon, brilliant and coal dust free. When she found that she was pregnant, his reaction frightened her.

"Oh, Maude, it's too soon." Seeing her face, he corrected himself. "Even so, just think, our son will be born in a place where there is no winter. We can take him for walks on the beach when he is a week old!"

"I am going home to Massachusetts, Cain. Our child must be born safely at home."

No amount of romantic entreaty could change her mind. The baby consumed her thoughts and feelings. Arguments about the danger of a sea voyage during wartime left her unmoved. She was untouched by news of a ship lost to submarine attack while on its way to New York. Reluctant and disappointed, he booked her passage for Boston. "The war will be over soon, my love," he assured her that last night, "and we'll be together with our baby in West Virginia."

In Maude's mind, nausea would be forever measured against the sickness she endured on that voyage, but safety greeted her at its end and her son was born, healthy and perfect.

Three more children were born in Holden in a frame house that shook every time the long coal train went by its tiny front porch. The black dust that became her enemy sifted through window cracks and came into the house in the creases of clothing and in children's hair. She boiled handkerchiefs, trying to get out the black stains where the family blew their noses during interminable winters of fog and illness. She carefully starched and ironed the cotton house dresses she wore but Cain never noticed.

She felt that she was growing old as he grew younger, always involved with a new group of schoolchildren. Often out with his friends, he left the house and children to her. Summers he went to Ohio University and took courses toward his dreamed-of degree.

Neighbors, who she knew saw her as stuck-up and northern, were only too happy to drop hints about his friends. The pastor's wife, her sole confidante besides Mrs. Lucas, to whom she wrote, did not tell her to disbelieve the rumors of women friends. They both understood how it was. That he had such friends was obvious to Maude but she had his children and was, if not content, very sure of her calling.

When her only daughter and youngest child was eighteen, Cain left for good and she endured the humiliation of the abandoned woman in a small town. As soon as she could she moved back to Logan and took a job as companion to Mr. Lucas's mother and father. She traveled with them to Florida and on cruises, even learned how to buy a little stock, judiciously, of course. When the Lucases endowed a home for retired clergymen in Florida they hired her to manage it.

Her suite of rooms overlooked the ocean and, for the first time in her life, she had her hair and nails done and her dresses came from a shop where the salespeople deferred to her. Everyone assumed she was a widow and she had never corrected that assumption. Now he had called and how cute he was to identify himself as her husband.

"Cain, this is Maude. What do you want?" The connection, to her dismay, had been instant.

"I'm on my way to Florida and I began imagining walking on the beach with you!" She shivered at the sound of his energy and straightforward pleasure.

"Is your wife with you?" She hated herself for rushing that question.

"Oh, we were divorced a long time ago. I told the boys, thought they'd tell you." She smiled realizing she had better things to talk about with her sons.

"I'm really very busy, Cain. I'm in charge of Lucas Hall now."

"Wonderful. You deserve credit. Your talent is obvious but Lucas knew about your character as well. So do I, Maude."

She did not intend to engage in banter but he was, after all, her grandchildren's grandfather. "I could have dinner with you Monday at seven, at the Davis Hotel. You have to wear a coat and tie."

"Wonderful! I'll be there. Good-bye."

"Good-bye." She sat for a long time, her hand still on the phone, until a spark of excitement was lost in indignation. How dare he? For her part, she would be dignified as befit the mother of distinguished sons.

A few weeks later, when she called Alan, her eldest, he was caught off guard. "Your father is here in Florida. He came here to see me. He wants us to remarry. What do you think?"

It was his way, she knew, to joke when he was unsure of himself. "Why not," he said. "It's nice for children's parents to be married." She was silent. He had neither given nor withheld his blessing.

"Sorry, Mother. Of course, it would make all of us happy if it makes you happy."

She told herself they would feel like part of a whole family again. Maybe her daughter would forgive her father.

The wedding dinner was, she thought, substance and symbol. Her daughter-in-law asked her what to serve and she suggested petits fours rather than a big cake. Cain chose snap beans cooked with onions, which made everybody laugh and hug him.

They lived near two of the sons in an apartment close to the library and church. She had a few pieces of fine furniture which she had collected but Cain had lost everything he had in his divorce settlement. They had fun going with Alan to used furniture stores and finding what they needed. Often they ate at a country restaurant before Alan had to go back to work.

Cain planted a big garden and all their neighbors admired his tomatoes and green beans. When he saw the rows of vegetables she had canned he said, "You were always the best housekeeper and mother I ever knew, Maude. I made a fool of myself." She tried to accept his repentance but a new fear was in her heart.

Atherosclerosis is a tricky thing. Cain had had recurring "inner ear infections" before their wedding. Now they knew his brain was being gradually deprived of oxygen. The family helped but often she found herself longing for the Florida sun and money coming in, not just going out. Then she would condemn herself as an unworthy mother and return to the cooking, cleaning, laundry, and the now gentle presence of the helpless old man.

There were strange moments when his mind seemed to clear, when he would speak to her. One day they were sitting in a glider under the maple tree and he reached for her hand. "I had so many children at school, Maude, I forgot how much our four needed me." And then he was gone.

The funeral home was in the old Lucas house in Logan. The Lucases had built a new house high on the mountain above the town where the stand-off between miners and owners had taken place before World War II had changed everything. The house was like the period at the end of a sentence of history, Maude thought, but for her the massive old brick house in the narrow valley would always be the Lucas house.

The funeral director, dressed in gray, directed them to gather in the old living room to greet friends. Her children were all there but they made it clear that they expected to see few mourners. Following her example, they were quietly dressed in suits and ties, and young (now nearly fifty years old!) Maude wore pearls, Maude noted with satisfaction, at her ears and throat. They had expected to leave soon after the few people who remembered them had been by. They were wrong.

People came in family groups and found old schoolfriends among the mourners. They were strangers with a disconcertingly familiar look to Maude, all speaking in the mountain English which to her would always be crude.

"I am Mary Jane Fogelsong, Mrs. Pridemore. You don't know, I'm sure, how much I enjoyed hearing you sing. Mr. Pridemore told me I would have to study to be like you and I did. I'm teaching music at the university at Morgantown now. When I heard of Mr. Pridemore's death I had to come and tell his children what his teaching and encouragement meant to me."

Young Maude, at her side, suddenly reached for the woman's hand. "Mary Jane," she cried, "we used to play together down by the tracks!" The two women embraced as childhood friends reunited do. Maude was in a daze as the line of mourners filed by. They remembered her and Cain but they did not remember her humiliation, her children's shame. Did her own children remember? She looked down the line and saw Alan take off his glasses and wipe his eyes. They were receiving their heritage, she thought. Their father was a teacher.

When she and young Maude got back to the motel room they shared, she said, "Maude, I want to be buried by your father here in West Virginia."

"Of course, Mother," her daughter answered. "The cemetery out on the mountainside is beautiful. I'll bring my children here to see it." She hugged her mother. "Now you take the first bath, and soak a while, like you never could in Holden."

Later, sleepless in the interrupted darkness of a motel room facing the parking lot and drapes that did not quite meet, she thought her daughter remembered enough.

The Evidence of
Things Not Seen

Miss Rose trudged up the steep hill, not so swift as she used to be, she laughed to herself. Anyway, the view from her windows was worth any climbing she had to do. She could see out over the valley and, in the morning, the mist lay along the river with the hills rising through it. There was something of immortality in that view. She did not bother to explain this to herself.

When she heard that Anne had a letter from Alice saying she was indeed coming for Christmas with Anne and Enos, Rose was instantly lost in memories. Miss Lena was still teaching when Rose was in school and after Lena's young husband was killed, Rose would sometimes walk partway up the hill with the teacher after school, neither of them talking. Sometimes she was invited to their house to play Monopoly or just to watch baby Alice. What joy she had brought to her mother. To others, too, Rose amended her thought. Alice had been loved.

As Alice got older Rose would see her in the early morning walking around the lower ridge on her way to visit with her grandpa before school. Sometimes she stopped below

Rose's house and looked out at the morning mist. Probably told her grandpa about that, they were that close. No wonder she made such good grades, all the way through graduate school.

Putting bookshelves, a desk, and two rocking chairs in one of the two rooms she had for Alice was her way of letting Alice know her privacy was respected, Rose told herself. But she would be pleased with some visiting.

Rose remembered making pickles with Miss Lena. How little Alice loved them! That child could eat more pickles than anyone they had ever seen, they said. People would probably talk about some kind of problem with metabolism or nutrition now but then they just laughed.

At Charleston Alice stepped out onto the just attached steps and onto ice. They hadn't been cleaned! A young man held her arm all the way into the terminal. "Thank you," she said, shortly, because she was not really that old. "You're welcome, mam. Have a nice Christmas." She looked up into smiling eyes that were, oh, so familiar. It seemed that nearly everyone in the terminal looked familiar. These were home folks.

Then she was being hugged and surrounded by two carloads of cousins who came to celebrate her arrival. "We'll eat at the new mall on the way home. Wait till you see it! They have a steakhouse and a Mexican restaurant both!" Anne's enthusiasm was not contagious. Alice had looked forward to homemade pickles.

When she had seen the rooms Miss Rose had for her Alice thanked her but said she really would like to eat with

Miss Rose and maybe visit in the evening. Besides, she told her, she remembered what a cook Miss Rose was. Rose's eyes filled with tears and she said, "You really are like her. Like Miss Lena." Alice embraced her and said, "No one ever gave me as beautiful a compliment as that."

It took a week for Rose to decide that the time for sentimentality was past. They needed help from an academic consultant and finding one with Galloway credentials was not an opportunity to be squandered on sweet nothings. She invited the Schultes for dinner and told them she had found a consultant for their meeting on school consolidation.

She sighed but indignation kept her from mental sagging. The schools in the county were not keeping up with the times and their children were suffering. She would use anybody to help, even Miss Lena's Alice.

John and Jane Schulte told Alice about coming to West Virginia with VISTA and deciding to stay. They loved the simpler life but recognized that change had to come. Over chicken and dumplings, home-canned beans and stewed tomatoes, pickles, and an applesauce cake with black walnuts, Alice told them about her year teaching in Changsha in China.

Then, as they enjoyed the percolated coffee, she heard the story of how they were trying to consolidate the three high schools in the county. "But," Alice protested, "people in this valley are completely different from those over the hill." Miss Rose and the Schultes stared at her. She felt the flush that suffused her neck and face.

"Those ideas are remarkably long-lived," John Schulte remarked dryly. Miss Rose put her hand over Alice's.

"We are still losing population here, Alice. Our young people have to leave because there are no jobs and they don't go on to college because we don't have the laboratories and books to train them." She spoke softly but Alice could see the respect in the eyes of the young teachers. "We have a plan for a high school in the middle of the county, here at Galloway, with dormitories for the children who live too far up in the mountains to get to any school, even with the three we have now. The state is threatening to take over our schools and consolidate them for us if we don't get a school bond passed soon."

"They can do it, too, Alice," Jane Schulte said, "they did it in two other counties last year."

"But you can take it to the courts!" Alice exclaimed. "There is a county unit system in West Virginia."

"We can't get people out for a school election, Alice. How could we go to court?"

"They'll go to court about sex education in the schools, Miss Rose," Jane laughed.

"Well, yes," Rose admitted, "but the preachers brought that about."

"Aren't the preachers willing to help with school elections?" Alice asked.

"We're afraid to ask them, Alice." Rose turned to look directly at Alice. "But you could ask them."

"Me? What do you mean? I'm a stranger."

"But you're a McHenry and they have been here longer than anyone. Besides, you have a fine education like the professors at West Virginia University. And your daddy would never have looked away from school needs, to say nothing of your Grandpa." She looked at Alice with affection but stern resolve. And, yes, hope.

"What should I do?" There was no other answer possible for Alice.

Rose felt a little guilty about invoking Alice's father, a father Alice could not even remember, but the children she had taught for so many years were worth any sacrifice on the part of adults. About that she did not equivocate.

Of course, the Baptists weren't much like they had been in Alice's Grandpa's day. She could remember him questioning every word the preacher said and arguing through long Sunday afternoons after dinner at Miss Lena's. But, as soon as she thought the old days wouldn't come again, she remembered Alice herself sitting and listening to the men argue, and Alice had laughed when she told Rose that her own daughter never took anything on faith. Odd word, faith . . . the evidence of things not seen . . .

The next day John and Enos came with a Jeep to take Alice sightseeing. "Do we have to go in this?" Alice asked, shivering even in her northern jacket.

"Afraid so. I have to show you why school buses don't always work here."

They headed up the river and took the left-hand fork. Tar-paper shacks and trailers were crowded close beside the road in the narrow valley. Children with dull, somber expressions hung onto makeshift porch rails or sat on the rocks that dotted their world.

"Buses can come here," Alice began.

"Yes, but it takes two hours to Guyan Valley High and even longer to Galloway." As he spoke they turned off the narrow road onto a timber trail that went up the steep mountainside. Hemlock boughs and the heavy leaves of rhododendron brushed against the plastic curtains of the Jeep. John leaned forward with the effort to keep on the trail. When they came over the brow of the hill another trail along the ridge led south toward Guyan. Trailers in small woodland clearings looked cold and barren, but curtains showed in the windows and paths to the privies were cleared of snow.

"Look down there, Alice, past that rocky cliff." Then she saw the unpainted schoolhouse sheltered by the cliff. A spring was green with cress. "This is like a dream," Alice murmured.

"Miss Addie Smith teaches up here and she does a damn good job even without a degree." John pulled into the clearing by the school. "No school today, of course." Alice was startled. The days of the week had lost their meaning for her. What would happen to her if she came back here to live?

"She gets them ready for high school," John continued, "but they can't get to a high school. It is just too hard to get there. That's why we want dorms. Did you know that Anne and Enos want to be house parents?" Enos was watching her.

"They would be perfect!" Alice exclaimed before she had time to modify her enthusiasm.

On Sunday, after church, Alice was eating dinner with Anne and Enos. "You knew what Miss Rose was prepared to get me into, didn't you?" Looking at her cousins, she found her answer in their smiles. "What do you think I should do?"

They were ready. The Baptists had to be convinced. That was the key to any election and a meeting was already set—an all-day workshop on education—for a week from Saturday and they needed a leader, someone who could be trusted by everyone.

"Oh, I know several competent experts," Alice put in.

"We don't need an expert. We need a Baptist, someone whose daddy was the founder of the American Baptist Church in Galloway." Anne grinned at Alice and Alice knew she was enlisted even though it had been a Northern Baptist Church in her daddy's time.

Rose lay awake, acutely aware of the woman, no longer young herself, working on the lecture upstairs. When Alice had told Rose that the lecture was hard to write, Rose bit her tongue. Lecture didn't seem like the right word for the Baptists. But what did she know? She had been a Southern Methodist for seventy years, mainly because her folks were all Democrats.

Funny how church, politics, school, even personality got all mixed up, consolidated even. She chuckled thinking that people who prided themselves on independence never figured this out. Alice had a fine education, an independent mind, but she needed more. She needed to consolidate her own parts. Rose hoped she would see the morning mist in the hills, something you don't explain, something you just know.

The night before the workshop Alice stayed up late finishing her lecture, using statistics about the results of school consolidation. Next morning she awoke before dawn, not sure what had wakened her, and walked up on the hillside to watch the morning mist, golden and heavy with memories. Below was Grandpa's house where she had heard so many stories. Maybe that was why she was not only a teacher but a writer. Suddenly she felt her heart beat faster. That was what she was looking for, not a lecture. She would tell one of Grandpa's stories. She ran back down the hill, excited and eager for the meeting.

They were all assembled in the church basement for breakfast when Enos got up to speak. "I *know* all of you join us in welcoming Cousin Alice. We will always welcome her." Everyone began to clap and smile. Alice grinned and told them to save their energy for the great biscuits and sausage the retired church members had prepared for them. "You won't see biscuits and apple butter like this in many places." She knew in that moment with profound wonder that she was one with them and that she did not need to understand. When she rose later to speak she was free, free in a way that she associated with writing.

"This morning I walked back on the Whittaker Hill and looked down on your houses and ours and thought of my grandfather. Most of you knew him, since he lived to such a grand old age. They tell me he kept singing in the choir until the last year of his life and never lost the pitch!" She laughed with her audience and wiped away a tear, as many of them did. "Well, I know what he would do if he was here. He'd tell a story!" People turned and smiled at each other in anticipation. "This is one of the last ones I heard him tell."

"My Great-Uncle Andy, you remember he was an itinerant surveyor and poet, would come to visit various relatives and stay undetermined lengths of time. Understandably it was a little hard on the relatives. Aunt Edna, in particular, was bothered by his habit of chewing tobacco and spitting on the floor. One time, when she heard that Uncle Andy was headed her way, she borrowed a spittoon from the courthouse and cleaned it up.

"When Uncle Andy got to Edna's he had a rhymed account of a schoolhouse tragedy that had happened in Texas the winter before. Aunt Edna carefully placed the spittoon to the right of his chair. As his mouth got too full for him to recite, he spit on the floor to the left of his chair. She discreetly moved the spittoon to the left. Then he spit to the right and said, 'Ednie, if you don't quit moving that thing, I am a-going to spit in it.'"

They all burst into laughter and listened as she continued telling them how her grandfather had moved from his beloved mountain home and the one-room school in which he taught when he realized that his children could not go to high school unless they moved to Galloway. "Not easy for a mountain family, as many of you know from experience." She paused and looked around the room filled with familiar faces and the few new young ones who were waiting to see where the old lady was going.

"John took me out to see in what remote places people live and how hard it is for them to get to school. He did not know it, but I knew those places because they are remarkably unchanged since my own childhood." John shifted in the pew beside Miss Rose. "Grandpa would find it familiar, too, and would know, as I do, that not all can move to town." This time she saw a lot of shifting.

"My daddy's family lived up the river and, when his sisters were ready for high school, they came and lived with us in town. Maybe there are homes here now that are available to young people. I don't know. Maybe you need to make dorms for them. I don't know that either. This I do know: all of you want a fine school for all your young people and there are people here who can give you a blueprint. But it will take all of us to make it happen. How I would have loved a library like the County Library here in Galloway! You should be very proud of it. I am going to make a contribution to it in memory of my grandfather."

She paused to share a quiet moment with them and then, grinning widely, she said, "Before you go to your small discussion and planning groups I have two things to tell you. If Charleston knows so much about your education, make them pay some of the cost of a big new school. And let's all remember that it takes a lot more than a clean spittoon to change people's habits."

Rose joined a group discussing how to get grant money from the state and maybe even the federal government.

Someone suggested raising funds from people in the county, charity, they said. Rose stood up with a look on her face that silenced all of them. "You know as well as I do, that children need to be in schools where all are indebted to the whole society, not just some rich folks who cannot be counted on to be constant. They are our children, our schools, and we can express ourselves only as citizens, all equal."

She sat down, knowing her words sounded like they were worth more than they were. She sighed, well, not everyone could tell stories but she thought she dreamed them, words that became a mist that made the harsh light of reality bearable. Not even Alice would get her to say such a thing, though.

Willy Mae Goes North

July 4, 1990

Dear Gene,

Well, here America is, 214 years old and still acting like a teen-ager. (Notice the hyphenated word: I am into that. Want to keep up-to-date.) Anyway, many raw-raw-anthems to you!

I'm wearing my Vermont Country Store tent jumper today. Makes me look even less than four eleven. The pink blouse fits right in with the smell of peonies that a breeze is bringing through the window. You and Daddy always called them "pinies."

My following the nephews to the upper midwest has been a blessing for them, they tell me. They can get to me quickly if I need them (which I don't) and they know I am all right (which I mostly am not. Who, I ask you, wants to be *all* right?). But they really have been dear and, at my age, it doesn't really matter that much where I am, does it? And there is always you—probably telling me right now that I just used really twice.

The little house they rent for me (I refused to live in a

high-rise with Lutherans or Methodists, the local choice) is on a sloping lot so I keep my hillbilly leg muscles in shape mowing my lawn. I have planted vining sweet peas (remember when you kissed me out by the fence that was covered with them?), nasturtiums, and August lilies so I can have a bouquet on my kitchen table all summer. (You always used to compliment me on the table I set in the kitchen.)

Well, think I'll bake some bread. Can't stand the stuff they sell at the store.

Faithfully,
Willy Mae

P.S. I am thinking of joining a writing group (they call it a class, which I doubt) at the Senior (better than Junior, I guess) Center. I can walk to the meetings and have breakfast at McDonald's on the way. It is uphill by Wisconsin standards from my house and that's good.

August 4, 1990
Dear Gene,

Summer was two days long. The wind is already rattling dry leaves high in the shag-bark hickories. They tell me winter lasts till May here but I think it's a northern version of bragging. Tough people, right?

I have to admit that the hickory nuts I gather here are better than in Tennessee. (You know, at ninety I can taste as well as ever?) They are large and seldom invaded by worms. I'll store them on my screened-in porch and use them this winter in apple salad and fudge. Only a few are dropping now but there will be lots more.

I went to the "class" and met my fellow writers. They range in age from sixty-but-not-admitting-it to my ninety-three. (Yes, I lied, but does it matter?) There is one retired preacher I have to fight off lest he minister unto me. How are you, he asks. I'm stiff as a board, half blind, and almost hairless, I say, and he backs off. He means well, of course. Don't know why I'm so ornery. I decided to write a story about him lightened up and the class liked it. Laughed till they cried.

The "assignment" was to remember walking. Didn't say who or where. I got to thinking of that preacher in a high-rise "home" downtown and had him walk to the Square where slightly less respectable people hang out. There he found a friend. The result is enclosed. What do you think of it?

Faithfully,
Willy Mae

You Meet Interesting People Out Walking by Willy Mae

At first I couldn't countenance my luck but gradually I became a true believer, confirmed. It began with Arch, whom I met out walking downtown, coming over and accidentally arriving at noon on Tuesday when Alice always has food out for me while she goes to her Guild. Arch ate everything in sight, which was normal, but I could tell something special was going on. I could tell as soon as he walked in that, even for Arch, he was acting odd. Finally, after three bowls of potato soup with homemade bread, he burst out, "Hamp, I can't tell anybody but you, and you have to promise not to breathe a word."

I said, "Sure," certain that Arch couldn't have anything to say that would be worth repeating.

"Professor Henry died last night!" Professor Henry wasn't really a professor, just an old man who had hung around the university for years doing odd jobs and inventing crazy things like flypaper to go on the floor to catch roaches. Definitely strange, but harmless. He lived in a room at the Downtown Y where Arch lives.

"Well, I'm sorry, Arch. I know you liked hearing his stories."

"But, Hamp, last night he didn't tell me a story. He gave me a time machine that he invented. It makes time stretch out. He told me he had lived over three hundred years and that was long enough." Arch looked wild as he continued, "Three hundred years—I think I was yelling at the poor old man. I told him, even he wasn't that old. Then he looked straight at me and he said, 'I have really been alive for three hundred years. Arch, just look in my trunk when I'm gone. You have been good to me and I want you to have it. The machine is in there.'" Arch had tears in his eyes. "Then he told me to go on down to my room, he was okay. This morning they told me he was dead."

"I'm sorry, Arch." I knew I was repeating myself but what could I say? The old man was crazy to the end.

"I went up to his room after I heard and they were cleaning things out. I said he wanted me to have the trunk but they said the lawyers were taking everything for probate. Seems the old professor had half a million dollars in the bank. Half a million dollars, Hamp, and they wouldn't even let me have that old trunk." Arch was standing, his knuckles white where he clutched the back of the kitchen chair, and his eyes were unnaturally wide. I felt a chill somewhere near where my spine reaches my head.

"Calm down," I said, "you don't know that there was anything in that trunk." I spoke slowly, with deliberation designed to give me time to think.

"But I don't know there wasn't!" This time Arch screamed. "And suppose there is a time machine and suppose a bunch of lawyers get it. Just suppose that, Hamp. Lawyers that have their time stretched out. Think about that. We would all be sued for breathing." He was getting more and more overwrought.

"Anyway, it's not your problem," I began.

"That's where you're wrong. It *is* my problem because I know what is in that trunk and I know who has it and I owe it to generations yet unborn to blow that trunk up."

Looking at him, it seemed to me that we were on the Damascus Road. He didn't want that machine for himself. He wanted to save society from unending lawyer time. He was a man with a calling and he was calling on me to help.

"Where is the trunk?" I asked.

"In a basement room at the Y."

"Is there much in that room?"

"Not much, it's behind the furnace."

"What if we started a fire back there and didn't tell anyone for a while? Would the whole building burn?"

Arch considered. "No, there's fireproofing in the floors. Of course, it's old. No guarantees."

Well, the newspaper came out the next day with a story about how the old Y burned and two courageous old men alerted the residents. The biggest law firm in town has volunteered to head a drive to raise money to build a new Y. Arch has a lifetime lease on a room in the new building and both of us get free use of all the exercise facilities. Probably will add years to our lives.

September 4, 1990
Dear Gene,

I have not repented that story even though you are silent about it. You have surely figured out that on my walk I saw one of those inane stupidly colorful machines by the bank that says "Tyme Machine." Makes my blood boil to see adults deliberately misspelling a word in public. As for the lawyer bit, we both remember the McCarthy stories we did, right?

Some leaves are turning. The writing class is between terms. I'll never admit it to them but I'm missing it. Even the "young" belle, Charlotte. Her children brought her out here from New York and I can't believe they are glad. She wants to have written but not to write. I got her attention by pointing out that it is as far from sixty to ninety years as it was from thirty to sixty.

You would find the teacher interesting. Gen is in her forties. Teaches at the state university and complains that the English Department faculty is mostly middle-aged men. I wonder what she would have done on the *Beckley Bugle* fifty years ago? She is after tenure and it is a high-pressure scene. She would say she is tense from trying to get tenure but tense doesn't describe her. I would call her desperate. I say she is desperate to find the courage to write. I believe she is a writer. There is something in me that she envies, I think. Not likes, just envies.

You might as well comment on Arch. I know what you're thinking.

Faithfully,
Willy Mae

October 4, 1990
Dear Gene,

Well, I have news about Gen. I was at the IGA Store one morning, sitting on the window ledge drinking free coffee, and one of the women from the Congregational Church saw me. Turns out she is the wife of the chair (not to say the table) of the English Department and a *talker*! Seems Gen's husband is an engineer with the local power company but has taken a leave of absence to teach in North Carolina. Why North Carolina? I innocently inquire. "Why, my dear, they are from the *south*. Didn't you know?"

"Shocked," I say. "Tell me about them." So she does.

They came up ten years ago and bought an old house near the campus (the kind abandoned by chairs twenty years ago). Gen is doing research in adult education. (I would rather have her using us as grist for her fiction mill than as dry statistics. But it doesn't surprise me that she is using us.)

Well, Mrs. Chair Nerdrum went on and on after my coffee was long cold and my legs were asleep. I hobbled home and wrote a story in my head on the way. Here it is. Don't comment, please, or worry the connection with the prof studying old age.

Faithfully,
Willy Mae

Aunt Doll's Quilt

Everyone along the creek came to Aunt Doll's house on Decoration Day. There was singing on the porch, some of the best quartet singing you ever heard. When the Toney brothers, lead and tenor, tuned up and sang "Precious Memories" you couldn't help but cry.

Dinner was on the ground. The women put their quilts down to spread food on. They opened their baskets and took out apple butter stack cakes, boiled greens, cornpone, fried apple pies, canned peaches, and fried chicken. "Everybody have some!" old man Kingery said after he had said thanks to God for the men who grew the food and the women who cooked it and the children who made everyone happy.

The men went from quilt to quilt and said they'd never tasted any food this good before in their lives. The children sat on the edge of the porch and tried to keep their new clothes from Montgomery Ward clean. Flies kept everyone slapping and wiping up spilled food.

Aunt Doll used to make the best chicken on the creek but she was too old to do much but churn butter and make quilts now. She sent Pearl to the well for butter that hung in the bucket down in the cool moss-covered place before you got to the water. It was good on pone and nearly everybody got to have some.

Preacher Wysong came over Blue Shoal Mountain about every two months and preached on Aunt Doll's porch or at the schoolhouse in the winter. It was a treat to hear a man who could talk so easily and say so little. Most people have to be careful about saying too much. He prayed for every person that had ever lived on the creek and then led the way up the hill to the graveyard.

The children had wreaths of velvet roses to put on the graves covered with pine needles, brown and soft. They struggled in the hot sun, their faces turned toward the wind that you could always feel up there. Their faces began to feel stiff as the sweat dried on them. Someone said this was the first year Aunt Doll hadn't made it up the hill.

Preacher Wysong said some words about the departed and the children placed their wreaths among the pine needles. Grown-ups murmured how pretty they were and wiped tears from their eyes. Little Nelle Toney asked why the graveyard was so high up on the hill.

"Because it is dry. Because it is dry, beautiful child," her grandmother explained. Others nodded.

"But, Grandma, how will we bring Aunt Doll up here?"

"We will carry her, child. In a pine box we'll carry her, when the time comes." The children were at peace as they skipped and slid back down the rocky path.

When they came around the corner of the log house, tight between the creek and the steep hill, where Doll had lived for eighty of her ninety-four years, they stopped and no one spoke. It was like a prayer. Spread out on the porch and hanging over the edge to the ground was a quilt like they had never seen before. It had patches of deep red and pink like pinies and velvet roses. There was a shadowy green all around, the way everything looks when it is bright but a cloud blows across the sun. Among the red and green there were brown and grey patches that looked like rocks nearly lost under all the growth. On each rock patch there was a name, a name of someone buried in the graveyard. At the bottom was one with Aunt Doll's name, just like she had signed it.

"This is a graveyard quilt. I have been saving the colors all my life and last winter was the time to make it up. For all these years, ever since my young'uns were little, I have gone down to the schoolhouse every Friday after I fed the men dinner to hear the teacher read. I wouldn't ever heard of Robinson Crusoe and that hard-working Friday or even of little Chad and the lonesome pine if it hadn't been for the teachers. Old Miss Hager is long dead so I can't thank her but Mr. Ferrell is here and I can sure thank him. This quilt is for you and your family, Mr. Ferrell. I won't need it."

She was right. Before the winter came we had carried her up the hill to the pine grove. There wasn't any preacher there. The Toney brothers sang "Precious Memories" and little Rose Ferrell recited the Twenty-third Psalm. The schoolteacher and his family took the quilt but they wouldn't use it. They said that someday there would be a museum for quilts.

November 4, 1990
Dear Gene,

No, I won't change graveyard to cemetery. I like for words to carry some weight.

Wish I could quit getting interested in people (I guess that is what made me a good newspaper snoop, as you used to call me). Anyway, Helen is a nearly blind member of our class, and her divorced son has moved back in with her. The other women in the class are horrified and say he will be the end of her writing. Maybe, I say, but not if she is really a writer. When I said that another member named Ardis grinned at me over their heads. I haven't told you about her. She and her husband ran a tavern, still spend time there. Her stories are great, Gene, really great. I go over to the tavern with her for lunch sometimes. We have thick hamburgers, hot french fries, and coffee fit for writers, not the Senior variety. She is the only person here that I would have you meet if you could only come.

Your watchful
Willy Mae

February 4, 1991
Dear Gene,

Flu got me and most of the class but it has been a good writing time. Wonder how you'll take to "Quilt" after you think it over. I sent it to a Wisconsin magazine and the editor sent it back saying I should make something happen. By the way, the Helen secret is out. Her son came home to die of AIDS. Are we modern or what? But it is very sad.

I've been thinking about what to do with my papers. The stories are all in a box in the basement. I wouldn't want anyone to see these letters to you. I'll burn them since you are long dead anyway.

But the stories might interest Gen. I'll leave them to her. She might have been my daughter if you hadn't married that nitwit Adelaide Booth. But we were both better off, weren't we? Friendship is a lot more rare than sex.

When I go downstairs to add "Quilt" to the box, I'll never make it back up that long flight of steep basement steps. There's a slow thump in my chest. Well, there are worse ways to go. I've always been trying to make it up to somewhere, haven't I?

Requiem aeternam,
Willy Mae

Just a Love Story

You will need to know Ellen Rainelle Gunning Phankuchen to understand the story I am about to tell. She is not thin but, then, she is not fat, favoring L. L. Bean for her clothes. She has a certain air, a style, you would admire, part church choir soprano and part earth mother. You will see what I mean.

We met during the Battle of the Bulge in a German woods. That is, I met her. The 101st Airborne had just dropped us behind the German lines and we had hustled into this woods to be quiet till dark. My pal, Tom, reached into his pocket for a smoke and a picture fell out.

"Who is that?" I asked, thinking the tomboy girl in the apple tree was his sweetheart.

"My sister Rainy," he said, handing me the picture that would change everything. I fell in love right then. She was grinning, but not much, and looking straight at the camera. Short curly hair was blowing around her face and I knew without being told that it was dark red. She was skinny but the promise was there. I was skinny in those days, too.

Well, we got the German telegraph wires cut that day

and my pal and I both went home without losing any body parts. I started writing to Ellen but, with Tom's advice, never called her Rainy. He was the only one who ever did that. The first time I went to visit the Gunnings and saw her I asked her to marry me and she said yes. Just like that and our fiftieth is about due.

She turned out to be a great cook, learned from her Maine mother who went down south to work and met a sweet-talking southerner and never went back to Maine. But she listened to my Pennsylvania Dutch mom, too, and it was a wonder just to have a regular meal at our house. Ask any of our four children and twelve grandchildren.

But there was something else, something I was slow to catch on to. It wasn't just that I was busy working for Ohio Bell. I knew there were things between mothers and children that I didn't have to understand. That is, till recently.

When we got ready to sell our big old house and move into a retirement-sized place out in the country by a pond, I had to figure some things out. Moving was more complicated than my heart attack. I handled that pretty well.

Ellen took to being quiet and getting tired when the family came. The children asked if her back was worse or if she was depressed. I said, "Hell, who isn't depressed at our age?" but I kept watch.

"We can't take a tenth of our stuff to our new house," Ellen said one day. "We might as well start burning." She had four big boxes labeled one for each of our kids and she was putting graduation programs, baby shoes, Scout uniforms, things like that, into each of them.

"The kids will be glad to get those things," I said, watching her.

"Maybe, but there's a lot more that they can't use."

I made up my mind to plunge in. "People around here have auctions," I said.

"Do you want an auction? Here? Auction off our household goods like we're dead?"

"Well, not exactly, but Mr. and Mrs. Holtzman out of Gallipolis would like to talk to us about it. They do auctions." Her face closed and she tossed me the haughty look I remember from her mother, before going upstairs and continuing her sorting.

"What a beautiful house," Jane Holtzman exclaimed, "and how perfectly it has been kept!" I thought that was it and Ellen would never speak to me again for inviting the Holtzmans but she could still throw me for a loop. Jane Holtzman went on, walking into the dining room, "You have a fortune here! This service for twelve in Rambling Rose will bring several thousand dollars."

"Really?"

"Yes, indeed," Mrs. Holtzman assured her, as they started up the steps. "And let's look at the books. They'll all sell, many for as much as five dollars." I could hear them talking as Mr. Holtzman and I went out to the garage.

Well, our auction is next Saturday. All the kids and grandchildren are going to help. The Holtzmans arranged for the Lutheran ladies to sell lunch in the yard and we have rented a Port-a-Potty. Don't want the customers to wander away.

Rainy has picked out a few things for the house by the pond and she has cleaned them till no old dirt will go with them into our new place. Mostly she has picked out new bright stuff that I like a lot. We laughed when it dawned on us that our old black cat's hair won't match the new carpets. "Easy to see," she told me.

You may be wondering why I have started calling her Rainy. It happened this way. We were walking around the pond at our new house and I stooped down to check a sharpened piece of churt that was partly buried in the ground. Indians used to live in this area. I looked up and there she was, with her still partly red hair blowing, leaning on a low branch of an old apple tree. I said, "I love you, Rainy."

She laughed, reaching for me. "I haven't heard that name since Tom died." We stood, remembering, and she fitted into my arms just the way I knew she would that day in Germany.

The Death of Alma Ruth

Two little girls, hiding in the broom sage in September sun, heard the old man whistling.

"Mr. Ferrell, Mr. Ferrell," they called, running up the hill to the pasture fence.

"Well, bless my soul, here are the children," the old man said, creases deepening in his cheeks where ambeer hardly showed on sun-browned skin. He bent and held the barbed wire apart for the children to crawl through.

"Can we walk with you?"

"You are welcome, but, if you walk the gas pipeline, you have to listen," he paused so they could hear the stillness, "and look," again he paused so they could shade their eyes with their hands and look along the pipe stretching over the edge of the pasture, "and smell, most of all, you have to smell."

"We will, Mr. Ferrell, we will."

They walked slowly, brows furrowed with concentration. "I smell persimmons!" Alma Ruth cried, and all of them hurried to the tree that leaned over the fence. Falling down among the warm dry grass, they began to taste the purple fruit.

"They are ripe. Let's take them to our mamas!" Ruby Louise was already filling her doll blanket.

"Here," Mr. Ferrell said, "here, sweet child, tie a knot on each corner and you'll have a basket." With his rough brown hands he tied neat knots in each corner of the blanket and helped the children fill it with fruit.

They scrambled under the barbed wire and started running down through broom sage. Ruby Louise turned and called, "Goodbye, Mr. Ferrell."

"Goodbye, children. Thank you for helping me."

"You are welcome, Mr. Ferrell," both little girls called, as they went down into the valley filled with echoes.

I felt old walking up the hill into late afternoon light and re-membering Mr. Ferrell. It was as if weights were tied to my shoes as I got closer to Alma Ruth's. My legs ached and I leaned to the hill too far—the way really old people do. Really old, I had to laugh to myself. What old is depends on how old you are. Really old had been Aunt Addie at fifty, Grandpa at sixty-two, even Miss Conza at forty. I guessed there were maybe a few people who would see me as old at nearly seventy. But Alma Ruth wasn't one of them, so I straightened myself up and looked up toward her house. There she was in the front bedroom window waving to me. I waved back and let the wind dry my tears so she wouldn't see me with my handkerchief out.

As I climbed up the steps to the porch Olaf came out the door. "How do you do, Ruby Louise?"

"I am fine, thank you, Olaf. It is good to have a doctor like you taking care of Alma Ruth. Mighty good."

The look in his eyes was that strange mixture of hurt and shame you see in the eyes of preachers and doctors. I have come to wonder whether God ever looks ashamed. "There isn't anything I can do, Ruby Louise."

"Of course there is, Olaf. You are doing it. You are keeping her comfortable."

"But I can't save her."

"I know that, Olaf, that is not for you to do. That is for God to do now."

"You really believe that, don't you? I used to go and pray to a special saint when people I loved were dying in LaCrosse. But then I learned that medicine helped more than my prayers."

"Well, now maybe you are back to prayers. It's just a question of when prayer is all there is."

He squeezed my arm with his free hand and kissed my cheek. "You are the best medicine I could prescribe for her. Good-bye. Call if you want me."

He didn't say need, he said want, and I knew he understood how hard it was for me to be with Alma Ruth, being always reminded that I was losing her. I couldn't even start getting my memories in order.

"Well, here is your mail, Alma Ruth. You are getting so much I can't walk up the hill with it without puffing." I handed her the *Hamlin Democrat*, some get well cards carefully chosen to say nothing, a letter marked "photos" from the preacher's wife, and a beat-up copy of the *Baptist Leader*.

"Why can't they put a cover on the *Leader* that will hold up in the mail?" she demanded. It was amazing how, even then, she cared about such things.

"You can't tell a book by its cover," I opined, hanging my coat in the hall closet.

"It's a good thing, Ruby Louise, if you're going to keep wearing that old coat much longer. Why don't you get a nice warm rust-brown coat? You still have a redhead's skin."

"I'm sure no redhead, though," I commented, patting my hair, mostly in vain.

"It is the skin tone that counts." Suddenly her voice was weak. I hurried to her.

"Alma Ruth, rest back on your pillows. You have been propped up looking out the window long enough." I busied myself straightening the covers and raising the shade farther so the sunset could come into the room.

"Ruby Louise, come here and sit on the bed. I have something to ask of you."

I went and sat facing her, holding her thin cold hand in both of mine. She began softly but her voice picked up.

"This afternoon I was dozing, half awake, I think, and I had this dream. I was looking down over the valley, watching for you, I think, Ruby Louise, and I could hear echoes everywhere. You know how it seems sometimes when the school band practices? Or the church bells ring? Well, it seemed like these echoes were voices and while I looked I could see the echoes. They had faces, faces of people I have known. People who are dead. And then, Ruby Louise, I saw my face. I was an echo." There was wonder in her voice but I couldn't go to this, this wonder, with her.

"Don't, Alma Ruth, don't talk like that." I was crying and I was mad at her. She put her poor little arms around me and said it was all right. Not everything needed to be said. And we sat like that for a long time till I got up to turn on the lights.

When Sophie Ann Rye came to spend the night Alma Ruth told me to go on home. Sophie Ann was good hearted and didn't know anything to say, a perfect nurse. We laughed and I got my coat.

"Good night, Alma Ruth, I'll be back with the mail in the morning and fix your breakfast."

"Wait a minute, Ruby Louise," she said, "come here close." She was talking softly but I knew she didn't need any argument. "I want you not to come tomorrow. John Mayhew will bring the mail. I want to talk to him. I'll declare he can get up on this hill like a man half his age. Have you noticed that, Ruby Louise?"

I said I had and all right I would wait till Wednesday but Sophie Ann could come for me if I was wanted.

"I know that, Ruby Louise. You have green tomatoes left on your vines and it has already frosted in some places. Why don't you make chow-chow tomorrow and bring me some? I love it first made."

"I'll do that, Alma Ruth," and she squeezed my hand. I knew something important had happened, something I didn't need to know, only to believe.

Jane and I drove up on the courthouse hill and got John Mayhew on the way to the church for the funeral. He always walked down the hill to the post office but not, as he said, "in his go-to-church shoes." It would be interesting to know when he ordered those shoes from Montgomery Ward. I told him our feet get longer as the rest of us settles. That is, when we get on toward old. But he said he needed shoes that hurt to keep him awake in church.

Everybody in the county was there for the funeral. We filed around the outside aisles and passed by the open casket while Charity sang "Precious Memories" in the purest voice you ever heard. You would have thought she had come from mountain people like we had. Alma Ruth loved to hear her sing. Said those old songs made her think of her daddy, so young dead in the mines.

Tears were so heavy in my eyes I couldn't see her as I stood before the casket. How can you say good-bye to part of yourself? You can't, and that's a fact. Alma Ruth will live as long as I do, I told myself. When I got back to my seat and watched the children from the Clearing pass by and wave, just like they did when Alma Ruth would start down to her house of an evening, it came to me. Nothing ever ends. There are new roads to take and corners to go around that we don't see till we get there. But each road and turn is right in its time.

I straightened up and listened to Preacher Pauley read the King James Bible.

"I will come again and receive you unto myself, that where I am you may be also."

"The Lord is my shepherd; I shall not want."

"I will lift up mine eyes unto the hills from whence cometh my help. My help cometh from the Lord who has made heaven and earth."

Preacher Pauley had asked me what hymns we should sing and I said there was only one Alma Ruth would ask for, "Take My Life." He said that was his thought, too, and he did just the right thing with it.

> *Take my life and let it be*
> *Consecrated, Lord, to thee;*
> *Take my moments and my days,*
> *Let them flow in ceaseless praise.*

When we got to the second verse, all of us hummed the tune while Charity sang the words so that they carried to the hills and back.

> *Take my hands, and let them move*
> *At the impulse of thy love;*
> *Take my feet, and let them be*
> *Swift and beautiful for thee.*

As surely as if we were sitting side by side, I turned to Alma Ruth and told her there was a beautiful new echo out there.

The women of the church had fixed a dinner for us but when I went in to the table and saw one of Alma Ruth's dried fruit cakes I couldn't stand anymore. "It was in my freezer. She made it last summer," Jane told me gently.

"I know, Jane, I know, but I have to go home now. Don't you take me. Not any of you. I want to walk. I'll be all right." I wanted to listen to the voices that they could not yet hear.

It was late when John Mayhew came. I had a good fire in the front room and the lamps turned on. He said he needed a cup of my coffee and a sweet cake. He couldn't eat the fruit cake and he couldn't eat the vegetables those young women cooked either. They made him think his taste buds were failing. Said the green beans were half raw and they had cooked peas in the fall when they didn't even have new potatoes.

"Sit down, John Mayhew. I just made some corn bread and I can heat up a can of my beans and slice an onion."

"Now, that is what I need, Ruby Louise. That is just what I need. I have something to show you."

When we got settled at the kitchen table he took some folded sheets of paper out of his pocket. "This is Alma Ruth's will, Ruby Louise. She wanted you to see it first. She had me write it down that day she wouldn't let you come to see her."

"That's like her." Why didn't I cry, I wondered. Truth was I couldn't feel sorry for myself. Not with Alma Ruth's words here in the room with me and John Mayhew reading them.

I want Ruby Louise to see this first and if she thinks I am wrong she should change it before anyone else sees it. I trust you, John Mayhew Grass, to see to this.

The Clearing has been good to me. I have sold my drawings and my quilts and my quilt patterns in a book. It makes me feel good, I don't know why, but it does, to have the Clearing up there. That is why I want to leave all of my money to make sure young people can take the classes up there and learn about what we know, or what I think we know. John Mayhew says that just the interest will make them able to have a school every summer.

My present to my true friend, Ruby Louise, is on a separate sheet and nobody but her can see it.

John Mayhew handed me a sheet of yellow paper filled with careful writing. I opened it and read.

Alma Ruth's Dried Fruit Cake

Dry your pears and peaches out in the sun spread on a clean sheet. Bring them in when you have to but take them back out in the sun till they are dry. Use apples or plums if you have to. Even get dried grapes at the store if you can't do any better.

Beat up 1 egg, ½ C brown sugar, and ½ C butter. Stir in 1 C of sour milk. Use it blinky or else get buttermilk.

Add 1 ¾ C flour, ¼ C corn starch, 1 tsp. mace, ¼ tsp. cloves, 1 tsp. baking soda. Mix and stir in ½ C cup cut up dried fruit. All pears is best and if you have them you won't need cinnamon. But if you fall back on apples put in some cinnamon. Add ½ C nuts. Hazel nuts from up on Two Mile are best but black walnuts from back on the hill are good. Hickory nuts are good in anything but don't use those walnuts from California. They take over any cake.

Bake it in a bread pan for half an hour. Check the center before you take it out of the oven. Medium heat is right. If you use Aunt Addie's old corn bread pan, double the recipe.

Icing—Cook 1 C brown sugar, 1 egg, 2 T milk, and 1 T butter till it has bubbles all over it. Add some vanilla if you want to. Cool it and spread it on the cake. Maybe, Ruby Louise, you had better go after the mail while it cools or you are sure to hurry it.

"An egg in the icing! I'll declare to goodness." I was just talking, trying not to cry.

"That's not all. She was afraid you would feel bad about not getting any of her money."

"Feel bad! I didn't even know she had any. Where did she get it, anyway?"

"Well, she got quite a bit from her quilts and things but she invested it carefully."

"Invested it! She never told me."

"I know, just like you never told her. She said to invest hers just like I did yours."

"You told her about mine!"

"No, she just knew. So I gave her the advice you gave me every time you consulted your apple tree." We both like to died laughing then remembering the day I admitted to him that the wisdom I came to sitting out under the old apple tree usually came after I read the *Wall Street Journal*.

"Ruby Louise, you know that my wife died young. She was not strong and losing Junior broke her heart. She was a woman to die of a broken heart."

"Not like me." It was just a fact.

It was a long time and a long way through memory before he went on. "I am very old, maybe our time has passed, but, on the other hand, maybe now I can speak for myself with the past put in its place. There is no use for us to be lonely, is there?"

"John Mayhew," I began but the tears choked the words that didn't need saying anyway. All the tears for all the loves lost poured onto John Mayhew's shoulder but he seemed able to manage.